How embarrassing!

"Doesn't this look *so good?*" I asked when I sat down.

But Jessica and Damon didn't seem to hear me. Whatever I had to say must have been a lot less interesting than what Damon was whispering about. I shrugged and focused on my lunch. I had to get used to being the odd girl out, I reasoned.

Just as I was taste testing the so-called vegetables on my plate, I heard someone walking up behind me. I glanced over my shoulder to see who it was.

"Hey," he said, with that killer smile.

"Hey, Jameel."

"Did you get my note?" he asked. His warm, dark brown eyes sparkled, and I noticed how curly and full his eyelashes were. The sound track in my head started playing something sappy and slow.

"Yes," I said dreamily. I was suddenly aware of Jessica and Damon turning their heads to listen. I straightened and stiffened. "Yes," I said again in a more curt, polite tone. "And thank you. But I'm not going to the Beach Blowout."

"But Bethel," Jessica interrupted. "We already talked about this. You said you're definitely going, remember?"

I gave her a look of death.

"She wants to go," Jessica told Jameel, ignoring the look. "She loves to dance."

Don't miss any of the books in SWEET VALLEY JUNIOR HIGH, an exciting series from Bantam Books!

Third Wheel

Written by
Jamie Suzanne

Created by
FRANCINE PASCAL

BANTAM BOOKS
NEW YORK·TORONTO·LONDON·SYDNEY·AUCKLAND

To Isabella Rose Vaccaro

RL 4, 008-012

THIRD WHEEL
A Bantam Book / January 2000

*Sweet Valley Junior High is a trademark of
Francine Pascal.*

Conceived by Francine Pascal.

17th Street Productions
A Division of Daniel Weiss Associates, Inc.

Produced by 17th Street Productions,
a division of Daniel Weiss Associates, Inc.
33 West 17th Street, New York, NY 10011.

ISBN: 0-553-48670-5

Published simultaneously in the United States and Canada

Bantam Books are published by Bantam Books, a division of Random
House, Inc. Its trademark, consisting of the words "Bantam Books" and
the portrayal of a rooster, is Registered in the U.S. Patent and Trademark
Office and in other countries. Marca Registrada. Bantam Books, 1540
Broadway, New York, New York 10036.

PRINTED IN THE UNITED STATES OF AMERICA

OPM   0 9 8 7 6 5 4 3 2 1

Bethel

I nudged Jessica Wakefield's arm. "There she is," I said. "Kennedy Middle School's star cross-country runner. She's the one to beat."

It took Jessica a second to figure out who I was talking about. She glanced around, the ten neon butterfly clips in her blond hair flashing in the southern California sun. We were standing in the Sweet Valley Junior High grandstand, waiting for the Tuesday afternoon all-district home track meet to begin.

All around us in the stands kids were talking and yelling, waiting for their events, watching their teammates, or just horsing around.

Below us on the track they were setting up for the boys' two-hundred-meter sprint. Kids were tacking down their starting blocks in the staggered start ahead of the backstretch.

"Down there," I said. I pointed, and Jessica looked.

Karla Cassidy, the Kennedy Terror, in Kennedy Middle School red and white, was using the track to practice starts. Not only was she great at cross-country; she was good at middle distances. I wondered if she had a special training regimen.

Jessica saw who I was pointing to just as Karla dropped out of her sprint and started jogging. She looked so relaxed, you couldn't tell how great her form was.

"Her?" Jessica asked, frowning.

"You didn't see her before. She was flying." I glared at Karla, psyching myself up to beat her in the cross-country later, then noticed someone sprinting up behind her.

He wore the SVJH team colors—blue-and-silver shorts and a tank top with his number pinned to the front. His dark legs flashed up and down as he raced up the homestretch in perfect form—arms pumping close in, knees high.

He crossed the hundred-meter finish line and rounded the curve. Finally he slowed, shaking out his hands, and turned to run back toward the stands.

I recognized him. Jameel Davis, from the boys' team. He joined this year. Sometimes in the hall at SVJH, I'd turn around and he'd be staring at me. He'd said hi a couple of times. He had lots of friends, and he seemed nice. I hadn't paid much attention to him.

I'd never watched him run all alone like that before, though. I'd just seen him in the middle of a pack of other boys. I knew he was good—

he had to be, to make the team—but I hadn't realized he was *that* good.

"Wow," I whispered.

"He's good," said Jessica.

"Better than good. That was fantastic."

She fluttered her eyelashes at me. "Fantastic, as in you *like* him?"

"Give me a break!"

Jessica leaned forward, slitted her eyes, and studied Jameel as he jogged toward us. Then she glanced at me. She was smiling a little too widely.

Uh-oh. Wheels were spinning in her head, I could tell. I looked for something to distract her.

Karla Cassidy had left the track. I couldn't see where she'd gone.

Jessica nudged me. "Check out that girl's nails," she hissed, nodding toward a girl dressed in a blue Jefferson Middle School sweatshirt. The girl's fingernails were bright green, with glow-in-the-dark, alien-head decals on them. "You never do your nails, but you should. You have great hands."

Jessica—queen of the short attention span! Sometimes I wonder how she can stay focused long enough to run a whole 3K race. "Spare me the Barbie brigade recruitment speech. I would never wear a color like that or put on those stupid stickers," I muttered.

3

"Yeah, and what a waste! A bright color would look great on you. I could do your nails for you. If I'd brought my polish today, I could do them now. I mean, how many *hours* do they need to set up for cross-country?"

On the track below, Jameel headed for the hundred-meter starting line again, knelt down, backed his feet into a set of starting blocks, put his hands right behind the line, leaned forward, lifted his butt, and took off as though he'd heard the starting pistol. Fast? Like lightning. I wanted to check my watch and see how fast he ran one hundred meters, but I couldn't take my eyes off him. He ran through the finish line and on around the curve again before he slowed.

"Wow," I whispered again before I could stop myself.

"Clear the track. Clear the track for the seventh-grade-boys, two-hundred-meter sprint," said a voice on the PA.

Jameel jogged back to the starting line and pulled his starting blocks off the track.

Jessica waved her hand in front of my face. "Earth to Bethel."

"Did you see that?"

"We have ribbons in the press box for sixth-grade girls, one hundred meters, for Tilton, Friesner, and Jens," said the announcer over the

PA. "Seventh-grade boys, first call for the two-hundred-meter sprint."

"See what?" said Jessica. "I hope Krebsy put some juice in the cooler. I'm feeling weak with boredom."

"Jameel. It wasn't even a race, but he ran so fast!"

Jessica smiled at me, that sly smile she got when she was scheming. "Don't look now, but he's coming this way."

I whipped around to see Jameel running up the grandstand stairs toward us.

He paused at the end of our row, looking around the stands. Then he glanced down.

Straight into my eyes.

He smiled this slow smile.

My pulse sped up. My face felt hot. He *was* cute!

Then he kept on running up the stairs.

"Hmmm," Jessica said. "Yes, we have an interesting situation here. History being made. Bethel looks at a boy and blushes. Mmm-hmm."

"Oh, shut up."

"Come on. I saw your face. You know you like him."

"Maybe a little." I could feel my mouth smiling. I couldn't stop it.

"Wait a sec," said Jessica. "What did you call him? Jameel?"

"Jameel Davis," I agreed.

"Oh no. This isn't going to work."

It was weird how her saying that made me feel. I didn't think: *Work? What work? What are you talking about?* I thought: *Wait a sec—what do you mean, it's not going to work? How would you know?*

"What are you talking about?" I said.

"I remember now. Jameel Davis. He's the seventh-grader who's so good, he's training with the eighth-grade boys, right?"

"Right."

"Seventh grade, Bethel. *Seventh. Grade.* He's a little kid!"

"Yeah, sure, like we're so much older. Anyway, who cares how old he is? Doesn't stop him from being a talented runner."

Jessica shook her head slowly. "So sad."

"What?"

"It's the first time I've seen you falling for somebody, and it's a little kid."

"Falling? What are you talking about? Can't I admire somebody without it being some kind of . . . something?"

She grinned, her blue-green eyes twinkling. "Nope," she said. "Actually, now that I think about it, it's kind of sweet." She poked around in her gym bag and pulled out a flyer. "Hey, remember this beach party Saturday after next?" she said, showing me the flyer. SVJH Annual Beach Blowout Saturday the 15th! Food, Dancing, Bonfire, and *Fun!* We'd all gotten flyers for it first period that morning.

"Sure," I said.

"You going?"

"I guess," I said. "Why not? I love to dance."

"Well, look. Why go alone? You could ask Jameel to go with you, and then you'd have a built-in dance partner," she said.

"What? Get out of here!"

"Come on. You know you want to."

"You're crazy," I laughed.

She turned away, still smiling that mischievous smile. "Hey! Ginger! Mary!" She waved wildly at some of the other members of our cross-country team, who were trotting up the stairs, carrying bottles of water. "Guess who Bethel likes!"

"Bethel likes somebody?" asked Ginger. Mary stared at me with mild surprise. She's one of the calmest people I know. Her looking surprised is the equivalent of somebody else going into shock.

"Shut *up*." I poked Jessica in the ribs.

"You'll never guess," Jessica persisted, scooting along the bench to get away from me. "It's somebody here in the stadium."

Ginger and Mary looked around for likely candidates.

"Shut *up*," I said again, scooting along the bench to get within poking range of Jessica.

She scooted away again. "And they just had, like, a moment."

"I miss all the good stuff!" Ginger wailed.

"*Shut up*," I said between clenched teeth.

Jessica laughed. "My lips are sealed," she told Mary and Ginger. "I won't tell you, but it's someone with the initials—mmmph!"

I slapped my hand over her mouth. Ginger's eyes got wide. Mary smiled half a smile and nodded in that serious way she has. She took Ginger's arm and dragged her away.

Slowly I let Jessica go.

She sighed. "Seriously, though. Would you go out with Jameel? I mean, if he actually asked you?"

"I don't go out with anyone," I said. "I've got enough going on in my life. I don't need a boyfriend."

That was easy to say. It was a lot harder to get Jameel's smile out of my mind.

"Bethel Runs on Clouds"
by Jameel Davis

She's fast and fine
So fine I lose my mind
She's like the morning sun
She's fierce but she has fun

Sometimes she's like a storm
Sometimes she's just warm
She hangs around my head
Like a ghost, only not dead

I wish she'd look my way
And hear what I want to say
I wish that she could see
Hey, Bethel, why not me?

Salvador

"What do you think of this one?" Elizabeth asked, setting a sheet of paper with something scribbled on it in front of me. Her blond hair fell straight to her shoulders, and she was wearing her favorite jeans and an orange T-shirt. She smelled like fruit shampoo.

It was Tuesday night, and my best friends, Anna Wang and Elizabeth Wakefield, and I were having an editorial meeting for our 'zine, the *Zone*. Brian Rainey, the fourth member of our editorial team, had to go to some big family birthday party in LA, but he said he trusted us to make the first cut.

Looking at these submissions, I wished I had a really big knife.

We sat at the big yellow table in the kitchen of my grandmother, the Doña. At least, the table was yellow last time I saw it. At the moment it was covered with pieces of paper—everything anyone had stuffed in the mailbox we'd put up at school for submissions to the *Zone*.

Across the table from me Anna stared at a piece of yellow legal-pad paper. She brushed her black hair behind her ears and chewed on the neck of her pink T-shirt. The frown line between her brows made me think that the piece she was studying must be either really bad or really good. Or maybe the handwriting was so bad, she had to squint to make sense out of it.

"Salvador?" Elizabeth wiggled a page in front of me. I blinked and tried to wake up. The squiggles on the paper resolved into a poem.

"Why are you such a space case tonight?" Anna asked me.

"Space case?" I grabbed the poem out of Elizabeth's hand. She liked a lot of stuff that I thought stunk. I prepared myself for the latest entry in the Make Salvador Gag Sweepstakes. Editing was harder than I thought.

"What's this?" Elizabeth asked, picking up the piece of paper I'd been staring at before.

Well, okay, *staring at* wasn't exactly the right words. More like *drawing on*. I guess it used to be a haiku sent to us by somebody in seventh grade. It had morphed. All that empty space on the page was too inviting. Guess I'd been sketching. Specifically two heads.

"This is really good," said Elizabeth. "It's different from your usual stuff."

11

Anna giggled.

"That didn't come out right," Elizabeth said. "I mean, your other stuff is good too. This is just so different. It isn't like the comic strip or your cartoons. It's portraits. Who are these people?"

Anna glanced over at the picture. "Oh, hey. That *is* good. Looks just like them. Have you been practicing?"

"It's my parents," I said. "And yes."

"Wow," said Elizabeth. She studied the picture. "Your dad is handsome. Your mom looks so pretty. They really look like this?" She glanced from me to Anna.

Anna nodded.

"You never talk about them," Elizabeth said. She raised her eyebrows.

It's astonishing how rarely my parents come up in casual conversation. Like, not at all. My Amazing All-Purpose Verbal Deflecto Shield works quite well.

I shrugged.

"Are they coming home again?" Anna asked.

"Yeah," I said. "Tomorrow. They'll be here for a week and a half." I wished I'd eaten something vanilla for dinner instead of the Doña's fire-breathing chili. My stomach was griping. It usually doesn't do that no matter what I eat, but—

I love my parents. They're great people.

Well, Dad is kind of bossy, but I'm sure he's a great person. I kind of get the feeling he would rather have a son who was a total psycho sports nut like him. I'm not exactly that son.

The other sad fact is that in spite of the best efforts of highly equipped expeditions with un-limited budgets and unrestricted amounts of time, the Search for Dad's Sense of Humor has never met with success.

But you know what they say. You can pick your nose, but you can't pick your parents.

Anyway, they're always happy to see me. At first. You know, like the first two minutes. While we're still hugging.

Before I open my mouth.

"That's great!" said Elizabeth. She glanced at me and Anna. I guess she noticed neither of us was grinning from ear to ear. "Isn't it?" Her voice faltered. She took a breath, then switched topics. "So where do they live again?"

"They move around a lot. They've been sta-tioned in Germany for the last year."

"Stationed?" she asked.

"They're both in the army. Majors. You know— my mother wears combat boots. Well, actually, she doesn't. She's a nurse in charge of part of the base hospital. My dad's in public affairs."

"Really?" Elizabeth asked, in this tone that

indicated she didn't know what to make of that. Well, who would?

"We'll probably do a bunch of stuff together," I said. "I don't know how much time I'll have for 'zine meetings while they're here." Since we only see each other a couple of times a year, my parents try to pack their visits with family activities. Okay, TV Land family activities. Like picnics, amusement parks, and clothes shopping. *Together*. It's a nightmare.

I mean, I appreciate the effort, but it's painful shopping with my parents. They load me up with dork clothes I will absolutely never wear after they leave. And I always feel guilty saying anything since I hardly ever see them.

But they just have no idea what goes on in the trenches at SVJH. How wearing the wrong shirt can send you right into the line of fire.

I looked at the picture I'd drawn. My parents were both smiling. Maybe it was a sign. This time we'd have a really good visit. Wouldn't that be cool? Maybe this time—for once—everything would go great.

I smiled. Then I realized these thoughts were familiar. I had them right before my parents' last visit. And look how that turned out. I don't know how many times I said, "I don't really like Disney movies anymore." My parents just can't deal with the fact that I'm growing up.

And something else bothered me about that last visit. Worse than family shopping trips, worse than G movies, there were the questions. Dad asking me questions about Anna. Like, what did Anna and I do all the time? Why did we spend so much time together? Like he thought it was weird that my best friend is a girl.

What was up with that? Dad knows Anna. We've been best friends for years.

And now I had Elizabeth—another friend who happened to be a girl. I wondered if he'd hassle me about her.

"Maybe we better do a lot of editing tonight," Anna said, interrupting my thoughts. "While you still have time."

She was being diplomatic. I knew what she really meant was, "Before you turn into a total brain-dead loser the way you always do when your parents show up."

Okay, Salvador. Settle down. One problem at a time, preferably the one you can actually do something about.

I looked at the mess on the kitchen table.

Charlie Roberts and the snotty crew on *Spectator,* the regular SVJH paper, hardly ever used submissions.

But a lot of kids at SVJH had something to

say, and Elizabeth wanted them to say it in the *Zone*. She was thrilled we had such a huge stack of papers to sort through.

Most of these entries sucked, though.

I hoped Anna would agree with me that we couldn't use every single thing we'd gotten, that we really had to say no to some of them—make that to a lot of them. Even though each of us had editorial veto power, I didn't want to be the bad guy here.

Well, not the only bad guy.

"Let's make three stacks, each look through a stack, and start building up our reject pile," I suggested.

"But—," Elizabeth began. She was so nice, she probably didn't want to reject anyone.

Well, who did?

I picked up a paper from the middle of the table. "Top Ten Ways to Keep Cool," by Justin Campbell, one of the ultimate SVJH cool-crowd creepazoids.

Sometimes you really want a nice, big rubber stamp that says *Reject* on it and a big pad of red ink.

Sometimes you'd like to stamp it right on some people's foreheads.

But first I had to read the list. Maybe Justin knew something I didn't.

I could sure use some extra cool when my parents got here.

Bethel

I slammed my hand down on the alarm clock. This time it skittered right off the bedside table and fell to the floor.

Maybe there's a limit to the number of times you can hit the snooze alarm before the clock panics. On the other hand, maybe I was just too mad and hit it too hard. I hate when the alarm interrupts a really good dream. I'd been running on an airport runway. I was keeping up with a plane that was taking off. And I was laughing as the finish-line tape broke across my chest.

I picked up the clock. The red digital numbers still glowed fiercely on its face despite my attack. For a minute they scrambled, and it looked like it was 2:17. But that couldn't be right. There was daylight outside. I focused, running my index finger under the numbers to get them in order. 7:12.

I panicked. Seven-twelve! What day was it? Wednesday! Definitely a school day. School started in eighteen minutes! Yikes. How many times had I hit snooze?

I jumped out of bed and threw on some clothes, laced my training flats on my feet for the run to school, stuffed my regular shoes and some books into my silver backpack, and ran downstairs. No time for breakfast. I drank a glass of milk and grabbed two granola bars and a banana. I could eat in algebra.

Mom was long gone—she teaches second grade and has to get to class before kids even think about showing up.

Dad was reading the paper and munching on a toasted bagel. He was still in his pajamas. He's a mystery writer. He works at home. He can stay in his pajamas all day if he likes. He usually doesn't, though. I'm still young and impressionable, and I need a good role model. At least, that's what Mom tells Dad when she thinks I'm not listening. A good role model doesn't spend his days in pajamas, I guess. I don't know why not, though. All I know is *I'll* never spend my days in pajamas. You miss the best running time if you don't get up in the morning.

"Bethel?" Dad blinked at me.

"No time, no time," I said, rushing past him. I backtracked. "I don't have time to make lunch," I said, jogging in place.

He got his wallet out of the pocket of his

jacket, which was hanging by the back door, and handed me a ten-dollar bill.

"Thanks," I said, and dashed out the door.

I ran all the way to school. It was a great morning for a run, cool and foggy, the air soft, smelling like the ocean. School wasn't far enough away, though. I was just starting to warm up when I got there.

I made it all the way to my locker and had opened my backpack to unload the books I'd need later in the day before I realized I'd left my binder, with all my completed homework assignments in it, on my desk at home.

I squeezed my eyes closed and then opened them again to make sure I was really awake. It didn't help.

Did I have time to run home and get the notebook? I checked my sports watch. No, it was already twenty after seven. No way could I make the trip home and back in ten minutes, even if I sprinted.

My locker partner, Richard Griggs, showed up to pick up his math book. I stood to the side while he shuffled through the top half of our locker.

"Hey, do you have a couple of sheets of paper I could borrow?" I asked him.

"Sure," he said. He ripped six sheets of lined

paper out of his spiral-bound notebook and handed them to me.

"Thanks. You're a lifesaver."

"Anytime." He headed off.

I took the books I wouldn't need until after lunch out of my backpack and started to stack them on the lower shelf, my shelf. I noticed a folded piece of lavender paper stuck through the locker vents. I figured it was a love note for Richard. He gets a lot of attention. He *is* pretty cute—tall, with intense green eyes and thick brown hair. If I were actually looking for a boyfriend, I could do a lot worse than Richard. I had seen several girls watching him the way girls do when they're working up the nerve to approach somebody.

But this note said *Bethel* on it, and I didn't recognize the handwriting.

I'd never gotten a note in my locker before. At least, not from somebody I didn't know.

I opened it. It was a copy of the Beach Blowout flyer. At the bottom there was a handwritten note: *Do you want to go?—Jameel.*

Jameel? I remembered that smile he gave me yesterday. So cute, it confused me because I never thought about boys that way. And I remembered the way he ran. Who could forget?

I smiled as I read over the note. Then I remembered how enthusiastic Jessica had been about me and Jameel going to the beach party together.

What if she'd told Jameel I was crushing on him and suggested he invite me?

How could she do something so *embarrassing*? Whatever I felt about Jameel, it was nobody's business but my own.

I bet she set me up! Was this her idea of fun? As in, *f-u-n-n-y*?

I wadded up the paper and stuck it in my backpack. This was so stupid. I could kill Jessica. I mean, Jameel was very, very cool. But like she said, he was in seventh grade. And like *I* said, I was totally not in the market for a boyfriend.

Anna

As usual the halls were complete chaos on Wednesday morning. I stood by Elizabeth's locker while she rooted around, looking for her math book. "What if those were their only copies?" she asked with her head half in her locker.

"Too bad," I said.

"They'll lose their work *forever*."

"Only the bad stuff." We had really narrowed the field last night at our editorial meeting. Out of sixty-two submissions we all agreed on eight. Salvador wanted to throw the rest away, but Elizabeth wouldn't let him. She wanted to preserve every poem about a dead pet, every set of lyrics stolen off rock videos on MTV, every ridiculous let's-write-a-story-set-in-the-*Star-Trek*-universe-but-call-the-characters-other-names story.

"I guess we could give back the ones with names on them," I said, though tracking down fifty-four people to tell them they were rejected didn't seem like a very fun job. "But some of those pieces weren't even signed."

"I know, but maybe we could figure out who they are by their handwriting," said Elizabeth.

I sighed. Loudly. Talk about impossible! Of the small percentage of people in school who actually wrote stuff down, how often did we see anything they wrote? What did she expect us to do, get handwriting samples from hundreds of people?

She closed her locker, spun the lock, and grinned at me. "Gotcha."

I had to laugh. I was always shocked when Elizabeth made a joke. I never expected it!

"Heads up!" a voice yelled from behind us. We both turned, and then a giant rubber band slapped Elizabeth on the forehead.

"Hey!" I cried.

She touched her forehead. There was a red streak across it.

I knelt and picked up the rubber band, then looked around for the shooter.

Brian Rainey crouched and shot off a rubber band. Hey! What was going on here? Brian? Cute, funny Brian, everybody's friend, just about the nicest guy around? He was way too cool to do stupid stuff like this! I turned to look where he had aimed. I was just in time to see Salvador whipping a rubber band out of his pocket. He leaned out around some passing girls to zing off a shot at Brian.

23

"Hey!" I yelled. "Which one of you shot this one?" I dangled the huge, red rubber band between my thumb and forefinger.

"Oh, thanks, Anna! That's my favorite," Salvador said, coming over.

He tried to grab the rubber band out of my hand. "Quit being such a jerk!" I said, and tucked it into my pocket.

"Anna, come on—I *need* that."

"Did you ever think you might injure someone with these things?" I pointed to Elizabeth, who still looked a little shell-shocked.

Salvador's eyes got wide and dopey, the way they sometimes do when he contemplates the object of his former adoration. Or maybe it's not so former. I can't keep track, and I don't try to anymore because it's so . . . irritating.

The first bell rang. Salvador swallowed, bobbed his head, and said, "Gotta go." He punched Brian's arm and headed off down the hall.

Without even saying he was sorry.

I couldn't believe it!

Elizabeth stared after him, her eyes as wide as mine must be, her mouth half open in surprise.

Salvador could act like an idiot sometimes, but I'd never seen him shoot and run. Something must be going on.

Then it hit me. "He's always a little tense right

before his parents get here. His mom is great, but his dad, well, he's kind of strict. Salvador's not good with strict."

"I've noticed." Elizabeth laughed.

"He still should have apologized."

Elizabeth shrugged. "So what are his parents like anyway? Can you tell me more?"

"Uh—how about we wait until lunch? First bell rang already."

"Oh, right. Hey, can I have that rubber band?" she asked.

I handed it to her, wondering who she was going to shoot with it.

Wait a minute; this was Elizabeth. She'd never shoot anybody with a rubber band, would she?

I guess Salvador isn't really anybody.

Jessica

Wednesday morning. Algebra. With Mr. Wilfred. For an hour and a half. Joy. Bliss. Paradise.

I lingered by my locker as long as possible.

Long enough to spot Damon coming up the hall and get that warm feeling in my stomach. I looked at him and sighed. Short, wavy brown hair, blue eyes, and that smile. So perfect!

Damon cut between people and came up to me. "Hi."

"Hi," I said. I smiled at him for a while, and he smiled at me. *This is stupid,* I thought. *We do this all the time.* I couldn't stop smiling, though. He was just so cute.

So when was he going to ask me to the big Beach Blowout? We got the flyer for it a whole day ago, and nothing.

Ask me, I beamed at him telepathically. *Let's get this over with. We'll both feel better.*

"Would you—," Damon began.

Yes! Yes! Just ask me!

The first bell rang.

No! No!

"Would you meet me for lunch?" he asked.

"Sure," I gushed. Then I realized I wasn't answering the question I was hoping for. Oh, well. Lunch would give him another chance to ask me. Maybe I could hint if he didn't get to it right away.

Bethel stormed up the hall and stopped to give me the ultimate glare.

Now what?

"Is something wrong?" I asked. I racked my brain, trying to figure out anything I had done recently that might have upset her. She hadn't been mad after the race yesterday, during which, by the way, we ruled. She came in first, beating the Kennedy Terror by three seconds, and me by ten seconds. Of *course* she hadn't been mad.

I hadn't seen her since.

"I don't have time for this," she said through clenched teeth, and headed to class.

Time for what? Since I couldn't think of anything I had done to make her mad, maybe somebody had said I'd done something I didn't do. I needed to know what so I could turn it around.

"I'll see you at lunch," I said to Damon, and ran after Bethel.

The final bell rang just as I headed through the door into algebra. Bethel was slumped in her seat, and I had to go to mine, which was in the back, pretty far away from her.

I stared at the back of her head, wondering what was going on inside it, but she didn't turn around.

Bethel was mad at me, and Damon wasn't asking me to the beach party. Did I have a sign stuck to my back today that said Pick on Me?

Elizabeth

By lunchtime I still had the big rubber band in my pocket.

I had thought about shooting it at Salvador, but he'd been acting so weird lately, I didn't know how he'd react.

My forehead stopped hurting after a few minutes anyway. And between classes I borrowed some cover stick from Jessica's locker and got rid of the red streak.

In the cafeteria Anna and I headed right for our usual table. "I still think that Jan Meier's piece was good enough to go in," I said. Jan wrote a poem, "Fat in a Thin World," that I thought was really good, but Salvador and Anna had nixed it since it was so heavy (excuse the pun).

"Maybe next issue," Anna said. "Can we talk about something else now?"

"I'm overdoing it, aren't I?"

She gave me a little grin. "Sometimes you're kind of intense," she said. She took a lunch box out of her backpack. It was a really old *Brady*

Bunch lunch box, only the Brady Bunch had Hello Kitty stickers stuck over their faces. Anna picked at one of the stickers. "It used to be my mom's when she was little," she said. "I thought it was so dorky when she gave it to me that I did some re-construction on it. Now I kind of wish I hadn't."

"I like it." I glanced around. "Hey, where's Salvador?" Usually he was the first one there.

"Huh," said Anna. She pointed with her chin at another table.

Salvador was sitting with Brian Rainey and a group of jocks I hardly knew. He was already halfway through a sandwich, talking and laughing and waving his hands around.

"What's that about?" I asked.

Anna cocked her head and pursed her mouth. "Parent-arrival syndrome, I guess." She frowned. "He's never been this weird about it, though."

I leaned toward her. "Can you tell me more about them?"

"Like I said before, they're nice. His mom is great, really fun. His father is really into sports. He did a lot of football in high school and college, and he won a bunch of shooting-competition medals. Have you seen the trophy shelf in Salvador's room? That's all stuff his dad won. I don't think he really gets why Salvador's not racking up the trophies too."

I watched Salvador chug a carton of milk without a straw. Then he stuffed the other half of his sandwich in his mouth—whole. He kept talking the whole time, and the guys around him were laughing. One of them punched him playfully on the arm.

Salvador looked at home over there.

I felt a strange pang just watching him. I remembered when Steven was thirteen and Jessica and I were ten, and he suddenly started acting differently. Like turning into a teenager made him some kind of pod person, replaced in the middle of the night by somebody else.

"Personality transplants," I muttered.

"He'll be fine. It's only temporary," Anna said.

I wasn't so sure.

Bethel

You can't spend all morning with steam shooting out your ears. By lunchtime I had calmed down some, but I still needed to interrogate Jessica. I scoped out the cafeteria until I spotted her.

Sitting with Damon.

I didn't want to talk about Jameel in front of Damon—way too embarrassing. It could wait until Jessica was alone.

I looked for somebody else to sit with. Ginger was at another table with Matt Walker, her sort-of boyfriend. Mary Stillwater was sitting there too, but she was talking to some boy I'd never met.

Everybody was in a couple! What was the deal? Did they pass out some list of rules about school social behavior and forget to give me a copy?

I scanned the cafeteria again, trying to figure out what to do.

Damon was a nice, quiet guy. He wouldn't mind

if I sat with them, and he wouldn't start spreading stupid gossip about me and Jameel either.

I took a deep breath and walked over to Jessica's table. She looked up, raised her eyebrows, and gave me a tentative half smile.

I scowled. *Be afraid, Jessica. Be very afraid.*

I sat down across from them, opened my back-pack, and took out the wadded-up invitation from Jameel. "Did you have anything to do with this?" I asked, tossing it across the table at Jessica.

She uncrumpled it, read it, and started to giggle and shake her head.

"Admit it, Wakefield," I growled. "You put him up to this."

Jessica took a sip from her milk carton and stopped laughing at me. "No," she said, "I had absolutely nothing to do with this. I did not talk to Jameel. I did not write him a note. I haven't even seen him since the meet. Promise."

I searched her face to see if she was telling the truth. She was, I was sure of it. "Oh. Okay. Sorry I suspected you, then," I apologized.

"But I might have done it if I'd thought of it," she said, laughing again.

"What is it?" Damon asked, leaning forward to look.

I reached across the table and snatched the flyer from Jessica's hands.

"Nothing!" I said quickly, and stuffed the flyer back into my backpack.

"Right." Damon grinned.

I lifted my shoulders and dropped them. "Sorry to be so touchy," I said.

"Hey, it happens." He smiled. Damon has sisters—I guess he's used to moody girls and their secrets.

I relaxed a fraction. "So it's okay if I eat lunch with you guys?"

"Sure," Jessica and Damon said in unison.

"Great. Watch my stuff." I got up and went through the line. When I saw the lunch entrée, I figured I was probably better off not eating at all—it was the weekly mound of white stuff we called It Might Be Macaroni. According to old SVJH lore, they cooked up a mountain of it two years ago and just keep scraping off a potful every Wednesday.

I was going to need energy for track practice later, though, so I loaded my tray with whatever the so-called cooks glopped onto it and headed back to the table.

"Doesn't this look *so good?*" I asked when I sat down.

But Jessica and Damon didn't seem to hear me. Jessica was picking at the label on Damon's juice bottle, her cheeks all flushed, and Damon was leaning forward, whispering to her.

I picked up my fork with mock eagerness. "Maybe they should host a food show here—*Gross-Out Gourmet*." I laughed.

Still, Jessica didn't even look up. Whatever I had to say must have been a lot less interesting than what Damon was whispering about. I shrugged and focused on my lunch. I had to get used to being the odd girl out, I reasoned.

Just as I was taste testing the so-called vegetables on my plate, I heard someone walking up behind me. I glanced over my shoulder to see who it was.

"Hey," he said, with that killer smile.

"Hey, Jameel."

"Did you get my note?" he asked. His warm, dark brown eyes sparkled, and I noticed how curly and full his eyelashes were. The sound track in my head started playing something sappy and slow.

"Yes," I said dreamily. I was suddenly aware of Jessica and Damon turning their heads to listen. I straightened and stiffened. "Yes," I said again in a more curt, polite tone. "And thank you. But I'm not going to the Beach Blowout."

"But Bethel," Jessica interrupted. "We already talked about this. You said you're definitely going, remember?"

I gave her a look of death.

"She wants to go," Jessica told Jameel, ignoring the look. "She loves to dance."

"Great," Jameel said. "So do I."

"Do you dance as well as you run?" I asked. When I heard what I'd said, I couldn't believe those words had come out of my mouth. *What is the matter with me?* I so did not want to say things like that out loud. I so did not want to even think things like that!

Jameel just laughed. "Wait and see," he said, and walked off.

"Hmmm," Damon murmured, smiling.

"Hey, Jessica," I heard Sheila Watson call over from the next table. "So Bethel likes younger men, huh?"

"Robbing the cradle!"

A bunch of people started yelling stupid things. I tried to ignore them while I mashed everything on my plate into a squishy, greenish yellow pancake.

This thing with Jameel is not going any further, I thought. Then I corrected myself.

What *thing?* We didn't have a thing.

Did we?

36

Salvador

They're coming, I thought. They're
coming today. They'll be here for dinner.

Sitting at the jock table during lunch, with
guys talking sports all around me, I felt jumpy
and strange. I really wanted to see Mom and
Dad. I could picture Mom's smile when she saw
I'd grown another three inches since the last
time we saw each other. A growth spurt was one
of the cooler things that happened to me, as far
as she was concerned. If I grew to be Godzilla
sized, she'd be so happy, she'd explode.

And I had the first issue of *Zone* to show
them when they asked what I had been up to
lately. It looked great, and I had to admit I was
proud of it.

I got this semisick feeling in my stomach when
I thought about Dad, though. Not for the usual
reasons. Sure, he was bossy—sometimes he acted
like he thought I enlisted to be his son just so I
could have the pleasure of obeying his orders.

But that was how he always was.

He'd told the Doña he wanted to have some father-son talks this time. Was he going to put the birds and the bees into military terminology? I could just imagine. "Son, when the enemy's armed and pointed at you, you have two choices. . . ."

There had to be a comic strip in it.

I glanced over my shoulder at Anna and Elizabeth, sitting at our regular table. They had their heads together. I wondered what they were talking about.

"Hey." Andre Washington interrupted my thoughts. "Let's go over it again. Who is the greatest basketball player who ever lived?"

"Michael Jackson," I said.

"*Bzzzzt!*" Andre cuffed me on the head. "You better be wrong on purpose there, dude."

"Duh! Michael Jordan." Even I knew that much. I'd seen him on commercials with Tweety Bird.

But the sick feeling in my stomach made it hard to concentrate. Even with all the help the jocks were giving me, my sports cram session wouldn't be enough to score points with Dad. I'd never managed to score points with him before—why should I hope to now?

Later that afternoon, right before we went to change for gym, I caught up with Anna and Elizabeth.

They stared at me frostily.

"I'm really sorry I'm really sorry I'm really sorry," I said.

"Do you remember why?" Anna asked.

"It's kind of a long list, starting with the rubber band," I said.

"Score!" Anna shouted.

I bowed to Elizabeth. "I'm incredibly sorry and remorseful that I hit you with my favorite rubber band," I said, keeping my head down. "I hereby offer you the opportunity to reciprocate." I straightened up and held out my hands, trying to look like a target. "Front view," I said, then turned around. "Back view. Take your pick."

Elizabeth shook her head and sighed. "Never mind," she said. "But I'm keeping the rubber band just in case."

"I thank you very sweetly for sparing me so completely. Okay, apology number two, lunch. You guys know my dad's a sports nut. I was doing research."

Anna and Elizabeth traded glances. "I'd give that about an eight on the excuse meter," Anna said.

"I agree," said Elizabeth.

"I think that's all. Right?"

They exchanged glances again.

"So we're cool?" I asked.

"We're cool," they said simultaneously.

Salvador

We headed into our separate locker rooms. While I changed clothes, some of the jocks I'd had lunch with started in on their sports quizzes again. Dad would not be proud. I got a lot of answers wrong. He was going to have a field day with me. His son: the wuss, the klutz, the clown, whose best friends are two girls. Great.

We headed out to join the girls for volleyball. I looked through the net at Anna and Elizabeth, my best friends, and mentally said good-bye to them for the next week and a half.

Jessica

"Hey, Bethel, there's that shirt you were looking for on Monday," Ginger said from the next row of lockers while we were getting dressed for gym. She pointed to a bench in the corner of the locker room.

"Cool. Thanks," Bethel called. "I was wondering where that went." After going to pick up the shirt, Bethel came back and sat down next to me to put on her training flats.

"Hey, Mary. Is that new guy you were having lunch with taking you to the Beach Blowout?" I asked.

Mary nodded and smiled a kind of I-know-a-secret smile. "His name's Craig. Matt's taking Ginger," she told me. "How about you, Jessica?"

Damon still hadn't asked me. I was pretty sure it was just an oversight. He probably just assumed we were going together. We weren't officially going out yet, but we'd been talking for a few weeks now. Still, it would be totally lame if I told them we were going together and then it didn't happen.

Jessica

"I haven't finalized my plans yet," I said, feigning confidence. I pulled my hair back into a ponytail, wrapped my favorite black scrunchie around it, and then tossed my head to make sure it swished right.

"I'm going with Bruce," Jan said. "Lana, do you have a date yet?"

"I'll find someone," Lana said as she slipped into her top.

"What is it with all these couples?" Bethel muttered to me.

"Bethel, do you have a date yet?" Ginger asked. She grabbed her ankle behind her and did a quadriceps stretch.

"No!" Bethel said a little too loudly.

"There's always Jameel," I said. It kind of flew out of my mouth, and then I wished I hadn't said anything because Bethel had been so touchy about it. But I knew she liked him, even if he was younger. After today's lunch it wasn't exactly a secret that he liked her. "He already asked you." Which was more than Damon had done for me.

If Bethel would just get over herself, maybe she could have some fun.

"Little Jameel?" someone hooted.

"The seventh-grader?" somebody else yelled.

"He's young, but he's cute," I said, coming to Jameel's defense.

Bethel gave me a total glare. "It'll never happen, so just shut up about it."

"Oh, come on, Bethel," Ginger pleaded. "He *is* cute."

"And he's almost as tall as you are!" Lana laughed.

"I am not dating Jameel! I am not dating a seventh-grader! I am not dating anyone!" Bethel exploded, her face screwed up in frustration.

"Bethel likes Jameel! Bethel likes Jameel!" everyone began to chant. I couldn't help myself. I laughed.

Bethel slammed her locker shut and stormed out of the locker room.

I remembered how enthralled she'd been, watching Jameel at the track meet yesterday. I wished she'd just admit that she liked him.

Sometimes she's way too stubborn for her own good.

Salvador

"How often do you think your parents get good Japanese food in Germany?" the Doña asked me as we arranged fresh flowers in about two hundred vases to put around the house. She'd made eight different kinds of sushi for dinner and even got a bottle of sake.

"You're right. It's great," I said. "Now they'll really know they're back in California."

She laughed.

That's one of the things I love about my grandmother. She almost always laughs at my jokes, even the bad ones. My parents almost never did. They just weren't on my wavelength.

My hands kept squeezing into fists. As soon as I forced them open, they'd close up again. I was feeling jumpy. My head filled with conflicting thoughts. *I can't wait to see my parents! I don't want to see them. We're going to have a great time. It's going to be awful. This time it will be different.*

My hands had worked themselves into fists again, so I couldn't even cross my fingers and make a wish. Like that ever worked.

"Take a deep breath," the Doña said. She patted my back.

I took a deep breath, held it for a minute, and blew it out.

"You have nothing to be nervous about," the Doña added. "Other than the Micky Mouse ears and Power Ranger pajamas your mother might have stashed in her suitcase for you."

I groaned.

"Or the football games your dad will drag you to."

"Doña!"

She giggled and rubbed my shoulder. "I'm sorry. I was trying to make you laugh."

"Well it isn't funny," I said, annoyed.

The Doña stared at me with her smiling brown eyes. She took my hand. Her skin was warm and dry and comforting. "I know, it's hard. Your parents don't know you as well as you want them to. But give them a chance. They might surprise you."

Just then a silver rental car pulled up in front of the house.

I took another deep breath and thought about running up to my room.

No, I ordered myself. *You're too big for that. Stay where you are.*

I blew out the breath and forced my shoulders to stop hunching.

Then I left my grandmother in the kitchen while I ran out to the car.

Mom burst out of the front seat. "Who's this? *Ay, mi!* My little Sally? When did you get so tall?" She hugged me tight.

It was kind of spooky but also very cool. I was tall enough now to look right over her head! I hugged her hard, and it felt good. She smelled great—she has this perfume she always wears, and I always forget about it after she's gone unless I'm walking through a store and somebody's sprayed it. Then it's like she's right there again. "I missed you," I said. My throat felt tight.

She leaned back and took a good look at my face, then she brushed her hand over my hair. "*Mi pequeñito!* No, I can't call you little one anymore, can I? So handsome!" She patted my cheek.

"Straighten up, soldier, and let me take a look at you," Dad said from behind her.

I found myself standing at attention without even thinking about it. He used to drill me on this stuff when I was a little kid. I liked it back then. It sure made him happy when I got it right, and that made me happy too.

Dad got this huge grin on his face. Huge!

Oh yeah! He likes me! This time it's going to be great! My hands stopped squeezing shut, and my throat opened up. I relaxed.

Until his next word.

"Football!" he said.

"Huh?"

"You're growing, son, you're growing. You're bulking up. You're ready for football!" He said *football* like it was a magic word. He punched my shoulder like I'd finally made it into the jock club.

He never listened when I told him I was a klutz. I like sports. I do. And I'd probably be good at them if I didn't trip over my own feet when I try to run. Balls are more likely to hit me on the head than land in my hands. That's just the way it is.

I was about to remind him of this for the five hundredth time, but then I thought, why not try a different tactic this time? *Strategy* was one of his favorite words, after all.

I blinked three times and heard myself say, "Maybe."

My dad slapped me on the back, grinning happily.

Score!

It was the first visit in a long time where he didn't get mad at me within the first five minutes.

We went inside, and all three of us were smiling for once.

"Marisol! *Mija!*" The Doña hugged my mom. "Fernando! How fine you look!" She hugged my dad. "Salvador!" She even gave me a hug and whispered, "I'm so proud of you! Everyone's still smiling!" Then she turned to my parents. "Wait until you see what I've made for your dinner!"

"Cheese soufflé? Wiener schnitzel? Fettuccini Alfredo? Borscht?" guessed Mom.

"Be patient," said the Doña, her eyes twinkling. "You have to admire the whole presentation. I hope you're hungry."

"I hope you know how to use chopsticks," I muttered under my breath.

The dining-room table looked great, if you like flower arrangements with pussy willows and chrysanthemums. The Doña had taken a class in flower arranging. It looked kind of spiky to me, but Mom liked it. "Oh, Mama, it's beautiful," she said, tears shining in her eyes.

The Doña served us miso soup in lacquered wooden bowls. Miso's cool because you're *supposed* to slurp it right out of the bowl. Fishing tofu cubes out of the soup with chopsticks takes a bit more coordination, so I just slurp them too.

Next the Doña set out dipping bowls for soy sauce, small plates, chopsticks, and chopstick rests.

Then she brought out the sushi, which she had arranged on a big plate to look like flowers. Mom and Dad couldn't stop oohing and ahhing.

The Doña made a special plate for me because she knows I don't like the raw fish or fish-egg kinds. I only eat the kinds with cooked crab or avocado and rice.

"Superior presentation, Doña," I said in the hearty food-critic voice I use almost every night, no matter what my grandmother cooks. "You are a cook-fu master."

"Why, thank you, sir," the Doña said, bowing her head.

"However the fish doesn't look quite dead yet. Allow me to kill it for you." I used a chopstick to harpoon one of the slimier-looking pieces of sushi on the big platter in the middle of the table.

"Salvador Constantine Northern del Valle!" my father interrupted in his you-just-broke-a-regulation-now-prepare-for-court-martial tone.

Oops. I'd forgotten how much my dad hated my clowning around. I let go of the chopstick. It looked kind of gross sticking out of that pile of raw fish.

"You will respect your elders!" Dad thundered.

I felt my face getting hot. About twenty quick retorts whizzed through my brain, most of them not very funny.

Without looking up, I removed the offending chopstick, picked up a piece of California roll, dipped it in soy sauce, and stuffed it in my mouth so I wouldn't be able to talk.

"Fernando," said the Doña, "Salvador respects

me. It may not be the sort of respect you're used to, but then again, Salvador is not in the army."

Dad looked annoyed and began to fiddle with his chopsticks. It took him a couple of minutes to stop breathing loudly through his nose.

I ate another California roll. I was really getting into being quiet. It worked so much better than anything I had tried before.

Mom smiled at me. "What kinds of adventures are you having in school this year, Sally?" she asked.

"Well, my friends and I are publishing a magazine," I said.

Mom and the Doña and I talked about school for a while. Eventually Dad calmed down enough to ask me a couple of questions. We finished eating, and I excused myself from the table to get some copies of the first issue of the *Zone*. By the time I got back downstairs, the table was cleared, except for cups of the Doña's favorite superstrong coffee. Not exactly the usual end to a Japanese meal, but definitely one of the Doña's traditions.

I handed out copies of the *Zone*. Mom laughed when she saw Elizabeth's menu. "I guess the cafeteria is still as horrible as it was when I went to school here!" she said.

Dad laughed at something, then looked

surprised, then laughed again, then looked upset. Mom kept reading and laughing.

Score! 2–0, I rule!

I think.

"It looks very professional, Salvador," Dad said. "I just wonder. . . . It's so . . . disrespectful."

"Sure, Dad. That's what makes it funny."

He stared at me for a long moment, his dark eyes hard, but then he looked down at the 'zine again. Maybe he didn't want to go ballistic twice in one night.

"Let's talk about our plans," Mom said quickly. "We're definitely going shopping. You need clothes that fit, even if you *are* growing quickly, Sally."

I guess they don't get the baggy look in Germany.

"And we want to take you to the Natural History Museum," she went on.

Again? True, it used to be one of my favorite places in the universe.

When I was six years old!

"There's a new Disney movie too. Have you seen it yet?"

"Not yet," I said quietly. Oh, boy.

"We could go to the zoo," Mom said. "Maybe we could do the pony ride."

"Mah-mm." I groaned.

"Marisol, don't be silly. Salvador's legs would reach the ground if he tried to sit on a pony," the Doña said, coming to my rescue.

Mom sighed and beamed up at me. "My little Sally. He keeps growing and growing."

I wanted to melt right through the floor, grateful that none of my friends were around to hear her call me "my little Sally," like the new sidekick for Barbie or something.

"We can go out for ice cream," Mom went on. "See some movies. Maybe we can take you to Disneyland this weekend."

All right! Now, that I could deal with. I hadn't been on the Indiana Jones ride yet. It has three different endings, so you can go on it again without knowing what will happen.

Maybe Mom and Dad would let me invite Elizabeth and Anna.

I looked at Dad while he sipped his coffee.

Somehow I couldn't picture Anna, Elizabeth, me, Dad, Mom, and maybe the Doña on our way to Disneyland together. No, wait. I could picture it, but not in a good light. In my mental image Dad was sneering—at me.

"The botanical gardens," Mom went on. "Heritage House."

Oh, boy. Two more of my favorite places to fall asleep standing up. We had seen them both during Mom and Dad's last visit too.

"Don't forget the games!" said Dad. "I've al-ready ordered tickets for the big university game. Anything good coming up this week at SVJH? How about at the high school?"

Just what I needed to make my nightmare complete.

I wanted to run out of the house, all the way to Anna's, and sit on her porch swing with her. I wanted it the way I usually want ice cream.

I opened my mouth to say something, but I couldn't think of anything tactful. Mom was looking at me with a strange expression. She was smiling, but she had this pleading look in her eyes.

I guess one good thing about tradition is you don't have to think. You just do what you always do.

"Great," I said weakly. "Everything sounds great."

From: BigS1
To: ANA3, wkfldE
Subject: They're hee-eere!

Greetings from Family Land. My parents think I'm six years old. They brought me a huge Lego set from Germany. Cheer: It has little knights in it. Jeer: No Godzilla. Follow-up cheer: I built a great big monster with the set and put the knights in its stomach.

Hope you guys have a good week while I'm busy playing with blocks.

Bethel

Richard, my locker partner, got to my locker before I did on Thursday morning. "Hey, Bethel," he said, "notes for you." He handed me some folded, colored pieces of paper with no names on the outside.

"How do you know they're for me?" I asked. I'd seen some of Richard's note traffic. Colored paper seemed more his style—girls trying to get his attention. Sometimes they even sprayed perfume on the notes, and that sure stunk up everything in our locker.

"I peeked," he said. "Sorry. I thought they were for me." He gave me this little embarrassed smile, slammed the locker shut, and took off down the hall.

I opened up the first note, the one on light purple paper. It was a poem. By Jameel Davis. I closed it before I read the poem, but I did see the first line. *You make the sun want to rise.* My heart sped up. My head felt hot. I wasn't sure what I was feeling—angry or excited—but there was this weird little twist to it that made the back of my throat tight, like I couldn't swallow.

I opened up the other two—pink paper and light blue paper. Two more poems by Jameel. I folded them shut again.

How bad were they? Exactly what did they say? I couldn't bear to look.

Acid burned in my stomach. Why was Jameel doing this? And why hadn't he at least put my name on the notes? Obviously he wanted Richard to read them. He wanted everybody to know how he felt about me. Well, I wished he'd consulted me before he started broadcasting his feelings.

When I get a real boyfriend (and I'm not saying I need one or am even looking for one), he and I are going to be the first people who know about it. Maybe we won't tell anybody for a while. People might guess, but we're not going to talk until we're good and ready. That's how it should be.

I jammed Jameel's poems into my backpack without reading them.

I couldn't pay attention during class. Everything seemed a little off center. I wanted to go back to my simple life before this not-so-secret-admirer stuff began. I could do without people teasing me too.

I wished I'd never looked twice at Jameel at that stupid track meet. Maybe that put some kind of spell on him. Like, if you pay attention to something, it pays attention back. Scary.

At the meet I had been looking at everybody and everything. Okay, I admit—all of a sudden I noticed Jameel, and then I couldn't take my eyes off him. It was like I had zoom lenses. And I felt happy watching him run. The kind of happiness you get when you see something really good. It wasn't like I wanted anything out of it.

I didn't think Jameel even knew I was alive. But now he was writing me love poems. I never did anything to attract his attention. What happened?

I didn't look at the poems until the break between first and second period.

Then I hid in a stall in the second-floor girls' bathroom and pulled the little pieces of colored paper out of my backpack.

I read the first one.

"ALL I ASK"
by Jameel Davis

You make the sun want to rise.
It needs to see into your eyes.
It knows you know the deepest thing.
Your beauty makes the first bird sing.

When you move, the music starts.
When you walk, you dance on my heart.
Please be kind and look my way.
Please give me the time of day.

Please just let me talk to you.
Don't shoot me down.
Don't make a frown.
Just listen. Don't give me the blues.

Just listen.
That's all I ask.

I read the poem again and sat there, thinking.
Just listen. Was that so much to ask?
Not really.
Unless he started saying things about him and me being a couple!
I read the other two poems.
It seemed like Jameel really, really liked me.
Once I had a crush on Tony Fortone, this actor on TV. I had this whole fantasy about him. His car broke down by the road, and he needed somebody to show him the way to the gas station, and I happened to be jogging by. So we ran into town together. He admired my running style, and I was really psyched that I could keep up with him. He knew I was different from his

other fans. I was completely cool and nice and didn't act all in awe and skeevy. I treated him like a person. Tony loved it. We went out for ice cream after he got his car fixed.

Okay, so that was my little secret fantasy when I was like nine or ten.

But wasn't this just like that? Jameel was crushing on me, and he didn't even know me. How could he like me?

His poems made me feel weird too. I mean, I'm the best person I know how to be, but I don't think I make the sun rise or birds sing. Still, having a guy say that kind of stuff to me, well, it made me feel good. And confused.

I folded up the poems and put them back in my backpack. Then I ran out into the between-class chaos of the hall—locker doors slamming, kids running, hall monitors yelling for them not to run, gossip flowing fast and loose from every direction. I hurried toward my next class until somebody grabbed my arm and pulled me to a stop.

Jameel!

I sucked in my breath. He had the most fantastic smile.

"Hey," he said softly.

"Hi," I said, glancing nervously at the floor and feeling way too self-conscious.

"Hey," Jameel again. I looked up, and he handed me a rose.

"Wooo!" somebody yelled.

"Bethel and Jameel, sittin' in a tree—"

"Young love! Really, *really* young love!"

I looked around. It was mostly the Eyeball Alley crowd yelling.

Lacey Frells stood smirking near her locker. "Can't find anybody your own age, huh, Bethel?" she asked.

"Can't you?" I shot back, but that was no good. Sure, she went with an older guy. But most kids at SVJH thought that was beyond cool. It just didn't work the other way around—older girl, younger guy.

Except maybe for the guy.

I glanced at Jameel. He was still smiling, like he didn't hear a thing people were saying or he didn't care.

The rose wasn't real. But it smelled way better than a real one That's because it was a red-foil-wrapped chocolate rose. Yum.

The bell rang, and we all jumped. I took the rose and ran, ducking into the classroom just as everybody else took their seats. As soon as I slid into my desk, I hid the rose in my backpack.

I didn't know whether to eat it or stomp on it.

Elizabeth

"Del Valle," said Matt Springmeier, volleyball team captain.

"Wakefield," said Brian Rainey, the captain of the other volleyball team.

Usually Bethel McCoy was one of the team captains, but the girls in track had a special early practice on Thursday afternoon. Salvador was the last boy to be picked. Gym wasn't his best subject.

I went over to stand behind Brian, feeling really weird. Salvador didn't call me last night to pretend to talk about homework. He didn't sit with me and Anna at lunch *again*, and now he was on a different team in gym. That wasn't exactly Salvador's fault, but it still felt like he was avoiding us.

"Gardner," Matt said.

"Wang," Brian said. Anna left the tiny group of girls waiting to be picked for teams and ran to stand next to me.

"I am *so* glad he didn't pick me last," she whispered to me. Anna was one of the shortest girls in the class and got picked last a lot in team sports.

"Me too," I whispered back. So far this year I hadn't distinguished myself in any sports. I usually had too much fun talking to Anna and Salvador to pay much attention in gym.

"I hate this game," Anna said. "It hurts my wrists."

"I know what you mean."

Miss Scarlett was giving us the evil eye for talking. The captains finished picking teams, and we headed for our side of the court. Anna and I started out in the front, by the net, and didn't get a chance to talk again until we had rotated through the positions to the back row.

"What's up with Salvador anyway?" I hissed, bending my knees and holding my hand out in front of me in case the ball came my way. "Did he stop talking to you the last time his parents visited?"

"Nope. This is the worst I've ever seen him," Anna said.

"Do you think he's okay?"

We watched Salvador through the net. The ball sailed toward him, and he bit his lip in concentration. Then he took a swing at it and sent it into the net. His team moaned its displeasure, and Salvador shrugged helplessly.

"Well, he's not playing any better. I guess hanging out with jocks hasn't done him much good," Anna said.

The first game ended, and we switched sides so each team had to face into the sun the same amount. I touched Salvador's arm as he passed me. "Hey," I murmured. "How are you?"

"Just swell," he answered. He didn't look swell.

"Elizabeth and I want to come to your house after school," Anna announced. "She wants to meet your parents."

Salvador's mouth fell open, and his eyes widened. For a second he just stood there like that. I felt like I could have pushed him over with one finger.

Then he straightened up and licked his lips. "No," he said quietly, and walked past us.

Anna and I stared after him.

Maybe Salvador really did have a personality transplant, I thought.

Jessica

"There she goes again," Lana said as we watched Bethel pull ahead of us. A whole lap ahead.

It was Thursday afternoon, and Coach Krebs was making us run two laps at top speed, with four-minute recovery walks in between. We had to do five sets before our warm down.

Mary, Lana, and I kept up with Bethel for the first two sets, and then we started lagging. Mary maintained speed better than Lana and I did. We kind of lost our oomph after the first one hundred meters, but we were still going faster than the rest of the team.

I knew I should be running faster, but my head wasn't in it today. I didn't know Lana very well, but I figured now was as good a time to get to know her as any.

"So did you find a date for the Blowout?" I managed to ask. It came out more like, "Suh dhyoof hind ha deet fer thuh blout?"

"Yeah," Lana panted back. "A boy I know

from private school. How about you?"

Why had I even brought this up? The word *blowout* hadn't come up between me and Damon yet. Not once. "Nope," I said. "I guess I'll go on my own."

Or maybe Damon would ask me. We still had over a week.

"Nothing wrong with that," Lana said. "Hey, look who's here."

We crossed the finish line and slowed to a walk.

Up ahead of us a boy sprinted onto the field and ran up alongside Bethel. I recognized Jameel.

"Whoa," said Lana. "What's he doing?"

"What does it look like?" I said. "He's chasing her."

Bethel put on an extra burst of speed, which was pretty intense, considering she was already a whole lap ahead of the rest of us and had been running for a while. Jameel kept up with her easily. But he was fresh, not at the end of a training session like she was. No way could Bethel outrun him.

I checked my watch. Our recovery time was almost over.

"Did you hear what he did this morning?" Lana asked.

"No, what?"

"He gave her a rose right in the hallway."

"No way!" I exclaimed. How could Bethel not

tell me something that major? The whole day had gone by, and this was the first I was hearing about it! Why hadn't she told me during lunch? Or while we were changing for track?

I knew there were some things Bethel liked to keep quiet about, the kinds of things other people told you before you even had to ask.

But a rose—that's big! And so sophisticated for a seventh-grader.

"It was a chocolate rose," Lana said.

Chocolate! Okay, drop it a notch on the sophistication scale. It was still very cool.

I checked my watch again. Our four-minute walk was over. I picked up the pace. Bethel and Jameel were running side by side ahead of us, talking casually, as if they weren't running at all. I wanted to get closer to them and see if I could hear what they were saying.

Lana poured on the speed too, probably for the same reason.

Bethel and Jameel looked so good together on the track. They both had perfect form. Why shouldn't they be a couple?

"Hey, Bethel, looking good!" Jan yelled from the sidelines.

"Hey, Jameel! Why don't you pick on someone your own age?"

"Bethel, throw him back—he's too small to keep!"

Bethel lost her stride and almost tripped. Jameel caught her elbow and steadied her. But she jerked her elbow out of his hand and sprinted ahead. Jameel stopped running and stood in the middle of the track, staring after Bethel.

I glanced at Jameel as Lana and I blew past him. His head was down, his hands on his knees. He looked like he'd just lost a race. Bethel was a blur in the distance, putting all her juice into getting far, far away. She looked like she was planning to sprint all the way home.

I'd always thought Bethel was the coolest because she didn't care what other people thought. Okay, people were teasing her, but she could take it. Even *I'd* been teased worse than that. So why was Bethel letting this get to her?

Bethel

I ran around behind the grandstand to do my warm downs and stretches. Krebsy came back to check on me but didn't do much more than wave before she went back to watch the rest of the team finish up the practice. I went through my whole catalog of stretches, but afterward I still felt hot, mad, and confused.

I hated that this whole Jameel situation was making me lose my concentration! I hated that now everybody figured it was okay to laugh at me.

Mostly I hated how mixed up I was inside. I mean, I *liked* Jameel, even more now than I did before I had anything to do with him. The poetry, the rose—they were sweet. And I liked talking to him. While we were running, he told me about his little brother and sisters, and I mentioned that I had an older sister, Renee. We had just started comparing parents when the girls on the sidelines started yelling at us.

Jameel was actually a very cool person.

But he was making me lose my focus. I came

pretty close to tripping out there, and I felt like a jerk in front of my friends.

I wished I could start this whole day over.

A cold shower was a good alternative.

I ran past the volleyball court on my way to the locker room. The regular gym class was playing a game.

"Hey, hold up Bethel," Salvador del Valle yelled from the back line. "You gotta hear this!"

I stopped. Somebody caught the ball and held it. All eyes were on Salvador. Sometimes he could be really funny, and I really needed a little comedy just then.

"You know we've been getting a lot of submissions for the *Zone*," Salvador began. Some of the students began to glance around nervously. "Hey, don't worry, Miss Scarlett only went to the bathroom half a minute ago, and you know it takes her ten minutes to do the surgical scrub down afterward," he added.

The gym class laughed and huddled around him.

"Today we received a song in our submission box," Salvador went on. "The lyrics are pretty easy. Everybody can learn it! Are you ready?"

Everyone nodded. I wondered if this was going to be a song about Miss Scarlett.

"It's supposed to be sung to the tune of 'Happy Birthday' so everyone can sing it. It honors one of our school sports heroes—Bethel McCoy! And it was written by another one of our school sports heroes—Jameel Davis! Are you ready?"

"We're ready!" everybody yelled.

Hello?

My palms started to sweat. I was ready! Ready to strangle Salvador and Jameel!

How could Jameel do this to me *again?* If he was going to write me a song, why couldn't he just sing it to me, not submit it to a school 'zine!

Just then the rest of the track team trotted by on the other side of the volleyball court.

"Hey, guys," Salvador yelled to them. "Listen to this!"

Of course, they stopped too.

It was kind of like watching a car wreck. I couldn't get my feet to move. Mortification and self-destructive fascination kept me pasted in place.

"Okay," Salvador announced. "Listen closely and join in when you're ready." He glanced up at me and winked. "Don't worry, Bethel, it's very flattering." He looked back at his captive audience. "Okay, everybody—here we go!"

Then he sang: "'She runs like the wind; she never gives in. She's stubborn and fast, and she usually wins!' Everybody now!"

Salvador was right. The words were pretty

70

simple. And as I listened in horror, everyone started singing.

"'She runs like the wind; she never gives in. She's stubborn and fast, and she usually wins!'"

My feet felt heavy, and I couldn't lift my hands or turn my head. I was going to have to stand here forever and listen to this unbearable song.

"Bethel!" Jessica's voice interrupted my thoughts. "What are they doing?"

I stared at her.

I could move!

"Are you crying?" she whispered.

Was I? I felt pretty numb.

"Come on, let's hit the showers," Jessica said loudly, talking right over the third round of the song. "You stink!" She shoved me toward the locker room, and my feet finally came unstuck from the ground.

Moving. I was moving! *Thank you, Jess. Thanks forever,* I thought. Miss Scarlett lumbered out of the rest room as we went by, and the song died immediately. I never thought I'd be happy to see Miss Scarlett, but this time I felt like giving her a big hug.

I stripped off my clothes and ran into the shower. Soon I was so wet, no one could tell if I was crying or not. Not even me.

Salvador

If you press a button under the diorama of the rain forest at the Natural History Museum, a line of ants carrying stuff bigger than their own bodies marches up a log.

This used to fascinate me when I was little.

Actually, the button doesn't work anymore. Neither does the one you press that turns off the "daylight" and turns on the black light so you can see how the wings of the weird, huge South American butterflies fluoresce.

It's too bad you can't turn the "daylight" off anymore because with the "daylight" on, you can see how dusty everything has gotten over the years.

Mom was drifting around on little clouds of nostalgic joy. "Oh, I remember this from when I was a little girl! It's so marvelous, isn't it, Sally?"

I guess the "daylight" switch in her head was still in the off position.

Next to us a little girl tugged on her mother's skirt and giggled. "Mommy, that boy's name is

Sally, just like my doll." The kid was about three feet tall, with short blond hair and pink-framed glasses. She bounced over to me and stared up into my face. "Are you a boy or a girl?"

"I'm an alien," I said in a metallic monotone. "The woman who appears to be my mother is also an alien. She has not learned how to speak like an earthling yet. She has great trouble remembering my assumed earthling name."

The owl-eyed little kid just stood there, staring at me.

"Sally," Mom cried. "Come look at these raccoons! Aren't they cute?"

Cute? They were dead and stuffed and kind of moth-eaten. I'd seen much better raccoons in the Doña's backyard. Juniper, the housekeeper, put dog chow out for them. She said that raccoons make the best pets. You can feed them if you want to, you can look at them when you want to, but you don't have to take care of them, and you don't have to worry if they leave and don't come back. Other raccoons will show up soon enough.

"Susie?" Owl Eyes's mother came over and took her hand. "Are you bothering this boy?"

"Mom, he says he's an alien."

She took a good look at me. "He's a teenager. Same thing," she said, and hauled Susie away.

Score one for Susie's mom.

73

The good thing about the museum visit was that nobody my age was around to witness my humiliation. They all had much cooler things to do after school than this. On the other hand, the place was overrun with little kids like Susie.

Dad came back from the rest room. "Are you two still poking around in here?" he asked. "Let's go to the Hall of California History."

"Look at the baby bobcats," Mom cried from behind me. "So cute!"

"Mom, they're dead," I pointed out.

She gave me a sharp look. "I know that," she said after a second. Then she smiled, showing more teeth than usual. "That's what makes them so cute! Mwahahahaha!"

Score one for *my* mom!

"This is supposed to be *educational*," my father reminded us. "You could at least read the signs on the displays."

Score minus one for Dad.

"But we read everything on the signs about a million times already. It's not like they put new stuff on them since the last time we were here."

Dad gave me a Look.

Score minus one for me.

We went to the Hall of California History and looked at a bunch of dioramas depicting miniaturized Native American life before Europeans

74

showed up. Tiny men wove roof thatch for dome-shaped houses and held spears poised to throw into glassy, frozen-waved water. Tiny women in grass skirts dried fish on wooden racks by tiny cotton fires or ground acorns for meal.

The first time I saw those dioramas, I thought they were totally awesome. I went home and tried to build villages in the backyard with grass and pine needles and stuff. I even got some little Dungeons & Dragons pewter figures and painted them and made them live in the backyard village.

Now all I could think of was how cool it would be if Godzilla happened to stomp by. I imagined the miniature screams from the little fake people, frozen in place and unable to get out of the way.

I laughed a villainous laugh.

"Godzilla dreams?" murmured Mom behind me. She put her hand on my shoulder.

"Huh?" I looked back at her.

"I know how your mind works," she whispered.

She smiled just the way she had about the dead bobcats.

Another point for Mom!

I'd forgotten how cool my mom is and how well we get along. Suddenly I wanted to hug her. But this was a public place, and it would be way too embarrassing, so I didn't.

Dad was checking out the display of Stone Age weapons: stone arrowheads, stone spear points, fishhooks carved from bone and shell. He always went to that display.

Mom and I headed for my favorite display in the whole hall, a skeleton curled up on a big whale bone. The skeleton still wore bits of what had been a leather dress and still had some hair. It was a Native American burial, and it was displayed as if it were still in the ground, like you were looking at a cross section of dirt with a grave in it and grass on top. As a kid, I had spent a long time staring at that skeleton, the little necklace of shell beads around the neck bones, the curled finger bones.

But the display was gone. There was nothing behind the glass. A sign below it said Exhibit Removed.

I looked at Mom, and she looked at me sympathetically. "I guess if I were dead, I wouldn't want people staring at me either," she said at last.

I found a bench and sat down. If they took out all the good stuff, what was I going to do while Dad inspected each and every exhibit?

Sleep came to mind.

How could I turn this whole experience into an article for the *Zone*?

What if, when people went to museums, the

exhibits watched them back? What if there were a whole race of creatures that lived in museums and observed human behavior? All they'd see would be people staring at them, or little kids whining and trying to drag their moms and dads over to look at something else, or people leaning close to the windows so they could pick their noses without someone else seeing them—

"Salvador," Dad yelled, "come check this out."

The industriousness speech, I thought. I walked over with dragging feet.

"Look at this," said Dad, pointing to an obsidian blade in the display case. "Isn't it beautiful? Such fine craftsmanship. All those people had to work with was rocks and deer horns and wood, and look what they made!"

"A belt buckle!" I guessed. "Or is it a hair ornament? Something to open peanut-butter jars with? The remote control of the gods?"

"What?" He wasn't used to me interrupting him.

"Uh, go on."

He stared at me for a minute longer, trying to eye laser me into submission—at least that's what it felt like. Then he continued. "If you just pay attention to everything in your environment, you will find the tools you need. You just have to be creative."

The speech didn't have quite the zing it had when I'd heard it the first fifty times. In fact, Dad sounded kind of subdued.

Half a point for me, I guess.

We went to the Hall of Birds, and I stared at a hummingbird nest built on top of an orange. There was one built in a loop of rope too. I like hummingbird nests the best—they're like tiny cups, with eggs the size of oval peas. The mourning-dove nest wasn't even a nest, just some eggs lying in the crotch of a tree with a couple of twigs near them.

There were cases and cases of bird nests, each with little fake eggs inside. After a little while you can get really tired of bird nests.

Lots of stuffed birds hung from the ceiling in the Hall of Birds, but the biggest one was the condor, Dad's favorite. It had a ten-foot wingspan—a huge bird that soared through the sky looking down on everything below, cruising for carrion.

Dad stared up at it. "King of the skies," he murmured.

I read the plaque for about the hundredth time in my life. "Hey, Dad, did you know the condor is a vulture?"

Dad cleared his throat, but Mom magically appeared before he could say anything. "Sally! You have to see what's here!" she cried, grabbing my arm and pulling me toward a new wing of the museum.

Whatever it was, I was up for it. Even if it turned out to be . . . cute.

Dinosaur skeletons! There was a plaster cast of a *Tyrannosaurus* skull with teeth as long as my hand and eye sockets so big, I could probably stick my head into one. The skull was almost five feet across.

"Wow! Wow! Wow!"

Dad and I leaned right over the railing together to get closer to that gigantic skull.

We stared at that head for a long time.

Then we both straightened up.

"Do you still have those little—," Dad asked, cocking his head.

"Yeah," I said.

Once when I was little and really sick, Dad got me a set of plastic dinosaurs. They were all kinds of stupid plastic colors—red, green, blue, yellow—and they weren't the most accurate toys in the world. We staged a whole bunch of dino battles on my quilt, though, with lots of growling and pretend biting. Dad let me be the *Tyrannosaurus* and munch down on his *Stegosaurus* and *Apatosaurus*.

"They're in a box in the closet," I said.

He chuckled, like he was sharing a little joke

with me. I guess you could call it a moment. Our first pleasant one.

We moved on to the *Archaeopteryx*. It was a cast of the Berlin specimen, a famous fossil with long, thin bones trapped on a flat rock. The bird got caught in the mud 140 million years ago, and you could still see the outlines of its feathers, which, when you think about it, is pretty awesome. I can't think of a single human being who's made an impression big enough to last 140 million years.

The label below the exhibit said scientists didn't know whether *Archaeopteryx* could even fly. It also said that birds were dinosaurs, the only ones still alive.

I felt a weird, prickly chill staring at that bird outline on this big, flat piece of plaster.

My dad put his arm around my shoulders, and we stood there and studied that fossil together. Neither of us said anything stupid. Pleasant moment number two.

As we were leaving, Dad bought me a new plastic *Tyrannosaurus* in the gift shop. It looked a lot more authentic than my old one.

In the car on the way home I sat in the backseat and stared at the backs of my parents' heads. *Dad and I could really get along if I would just shut up,* I thought. Of course, it would help if he shut up too, but that wasn't going to happen, was it?

I thought about the kinds of arguments I always had with my dad. The stupidest thing about them was they always sounded the same, and neither of us ever changed our minds.

Maybe this time we could just not argue.

I jumped the *Tyrannosaurus* around on the top of the front seat, making growling noises. "*Rrrr,* I want your ear," I said, bouncing it onto Mom's shoulder. "Yum."

She laughed.

"Straighten up, soldier," Dad snapped.

I responded automatically, dropping back into my seat and pulling away my arm. The *T. Rex* hit the floor.

So much for pleasant moments.

From: BigS1
To: ANA3, wkfldE
Subject: I can't believe I did that

Thursday Night
   You guys, I cannot believe how lame
I was today. I need a T-shirt that
says I'm Sorry. I'd sure wear it a
lot. Anyway, I'm going to make it up
to you. Please please please meet me
for lunch tomorrow, and I'll try to
explain.

Elizabeth

"That dumb El Salvador made her cry. If you ever tell anyone that, though, I'll never speak to you again," Jessica told me as we waited at the bus stop on Friday morning.

"Salvador made Bethel cry?" After the brush-off he gave me and Anna yesterday, I *wanted* to be surprised that Salvador would hurt someone else's feelings, but I wasn't. My friend was turning into a stranger. "How? What did he do?"

"He got the whole gym class to sing this stupid song yesterday."

I gulped.

But I'd been there. I'd even sung along! I had no idea that the song would upset Bethel. It was a *nice* song. It was basically all about what a good runner Bethel was, right? And basically, I had been happy to see Salvador act silly, like his old, pre-parental-visit self that I hadn't even noticed how Bethel had reacted.

Basically I had been totally thoughtless.

"So she didn't like the song?" I guessed. I felt

83

sick to my stomach. Why hadn't I been paying attention?

Jessica's eyes narrowed to slits. "You were singing too—I saw you! How *could* you, Lizzie?"

"Honestly, Jess, I didn't realize it was mean," I protested. I wondered if Salvador knew it was mean. Had he done it on purpose?

No. No way could he change that much in three days. I had to have faith in my friend.

"It was a mistake," I insisted. "Salvador was just having fun."

"Well, tell El Salvador to leave Bethel alone, all right?" Jessica said.

"I will," I promised, as if I had anything to do with what Salvador did or didn't do these days.

Dear Bethel,

Sorry I messed up your sprints yesterday. I didn't mean to, honest.

I wish the girls' and boys' team practiced together all the time.

Anyway, see you at the Beach Blowout, right?

—Jameel

Bethel

On Friday morning I opened my locker door, and a light blue piece of paper fluttered out.

I had run all the way to school so I could check my locker before Richard got there. I'd scolded myself for being paranoid, but now I was glad I'd done it. The note was folded and unlabeled, but as soon as I opened it, I recognized Jameel's handwriting.

First bell rang. I slammed my locker shut and headed toward algebra class. Salvador del Valle walked by. "More fan mail?" he asked, glancing at the note in my hand.

I crushed Jameel's invitation in my fist and took a step toward Salvador. I wasn't sure if I was going to smack him or just try to stare him down.

He held up his hands. "Hey. Hey. I'm sorry about what happened in gym yesterday. I didn't mean anything against you, Bethel. I just thought it was funny."

"Oh, really?" I demanded. "Well, you have a funny idea of what's funny."

"I know," Salvador said. "Anyway, it was a nice song—what was so bad about it?"

"None of your business," I snapped.

"Fine. Okay, I'm sorry." Salvador waved and disappeared into the river of students.

I sat through my morning classes, stewing. I couldn't take any more teasing and humiliation. I had to tell Jameel to stop this nonsense once and for all.

I resolved to go looking for him at lunchtime. But Jameel found me first. When I headed back to my locker to get my lunch, he was leaning against it.

"You and I have got to talk," I said.

"Anytime, anywhere," he said, and smiled at me.

For a moment I was hypnotized by his incredibly cute smile.

Stop it, Bethel!

"Right here, right now." I opened my locker, and a pink piece of paper fluttered out. So that was what he was doing here! I felt my face get hot, and I shoved the note in my backpack without looking at it.

I whirled around. "You have to stop this stuff, Jameel!"

"Why?" he asked, still smiling.

"Everybody's making fun of us. It's messing up my practices. I don't want a boyfriend, especially not

87

one who sends a poem or a song or whatever about me to some magazine without even telling me."

"Sends a poem to—did the *Zone* come out already? I thought they'd at least tell me if they were going to publish them."

"'*Them*'?"

Jameel looked at the floor and bit his lower lip. "I don't know if the poems are any good. They're the first ones I ever wrote. I thought if I sent them to the *Zone*, one of the editors would tell me if they were all right. As poems, I mean. I didn't exactly want to turn them in for English class."

I had a horrible sinking feeling in my stomach. He had sent other poems about me to the *Zone*? Salvador, whom I now knew as Supreme Evil on Earth, had access to all this material? I wasn't sure how much more of this I could take. "How many of them are there?"

"Six or seven. I forget. Maybe eight or nine. I didn't turn them all in at the same time."

"Jameel." I took a deep breath. "How long have you been writing poems?"

"About a month."

"Are they all about me?"

He looked up into my face and smiled this kind of dopey smile. "Uh-huh."

"You've been writing poems about me for a *month*?" I couldn't believe this!

"I saw you run at the district track meet a month ago. I don't know what happened. I just—" He swallowed. "I couldn't stop thinking about you."

I hung on my locker door to steady myself. In a way, I knew what he meant. Hadn't I been obsessing about him too? "But how can you write about me when you hardly even know me?" I protested.

"But I want to know you. Just tell me everything," he insisted.

I sighed, reached into my locker, and grabbed my brown bag lunch. Jameel walked beside me to the cafeteria.

"How'd you get started in track?" he asked.

"My sister ran first," I explained. "Renee's good at everything. She's beautiful, a genius, and gets all A's. She's practically perfect. She got a full track scholarship at Brown. I'm not as good a student, but I can run just as well. She taught me a lot."

I glanced anxiously at Jameel, wondering what he thought. He just nodded. "Cool," he said.

"How about you?" I asked him.

"My dad did a lot of sports in college. Sports and journalism; that's what he studied. Now he's a sports reporter on the *Sweet Valley Times*. When I was really little, he got me to try a bunch of different sports. I like track and field the best, and swimming too." He shrugged.

The more I got to know about Jameel, the better I

liked him. I didn't want this conversation to end, but we were about to walk into a serious reality check. I felt my body tensing up as I pushed open the doors to the cafeteria. We walked into a wall of sound. I expected everyone to stop talking and eating as soon as we walked in. But no one seemed to notice us.

Maybe it would be all right. Maybe nobody cared anymore. Maybe I could just talk to Jameel like a normal person, even though he was a seventh-grader, and nothing would happen.

Jameel picked up a tray and headed for the cafeteria line. I followed, even though I had my own lunch.

"What's your favorite color?" Jameel asked. He held out his tray. Geriatric pizza with shriveled pepperoni on top, swimming in grease and burned crust. I felt sorry for his stomach.

"Blue," I said. "Actually, clear, light blue. Aquamarine, if you want to get technical. What about you?"

"Red." He grinned at me, and I couldn't help smiling back. We came to the end of the line, and Jameel paid the cashier. We turned around to look for a place to sit.

We'd been sighted. Sheila Watson was staring at us and talking to the girl next to her, an ugly smile on her face. Most of my track team was sitting at a table together, and some of them were grinning knowingly at me.

90

I was wrong. The problem wasn't over. Maybe it would never end.

Before I'd gone to my locker to get my lunch, I had made the decision to tell Jameel to leave me alone once and for all. Just because we'd talked didn't mean I'd changed my mind.

I looked at the wall, past Jameel's right shoulder. "Okay," I said. "See you." Then I brushed past him.

Jameel touched my arm. His hand felt warm. "But—"

I turned to glare at him, and his brown eyes were soft—serious and kind at the same time.

"Oh, Bethel, don't leave me!" Sheila Watson said dramatically, and everyone at her table laughed.

I took a deep breath.

"Go on," I hissed at Jameel. "Get lost."

It was one of those moments when a bunch of conversations come to a stop at the same time, like somebody's conducting them and he holds the baton still.

Jameel's eyes got wide, and his face fell. Then he dropped his hand from my arm and walked away.

Shame flooded through me. My stomach burned, and I felt like I was going to throw up. How could I be so mean? Jameel had never been anything but nice to me.

I turned and walked out of the cafeteria. I wasn't hungry anymore.

Anna

On Friday, Elizabeth and I watched Salvador make his way through the lunch line.

Despite the e-mail last night, I wondered if he'd go sit with the jocks today, the way he had the last two days.

"Maybe he'll explain," Elizabeth said hopefully.

"It better be good," I said, and then frowned. "I guess we should cut him more slack. If you saw Sal with his dad, you'd understand."

"You didn't tell me it was that bad."

"I thought you should form your own first impressions, but if he's never even going to introduce you to them . . ."

Salvador brought his tray over to the table, set it down, and collapsed into a chair. He heaved a big sigh. "Kill me now."

I punched him lightly on the shoulder.

"Ow," he said. "Okay. Now I feel better."

"What's *wrong* with you?" I demanded.

Salvador gripped his head with both hands.

He groaned. "I wish I could explain it, but even if I could, I feel like it's too stupid."

"You don't want me to meet your parents," Elizabeth said. "You're ashamed of me?"

"What?" He had this panicky look in his eyes when he glanced at her.

How could anybody be ashamed of Elizabeth? I wondered.

"It's not that," Salvador said guiltily.

"You're ashamed of your parents?" Elizabeth guessed.

He sighed and started picking mystery meat off his pizza. Or maybe it was mystery something else. It was too shriveled to tell. "It's a little more complicated than that."

"So? Tell us," I said.

His mouth tightened. "I can't. All I can do is apologize as many times as you want and hope you'll eventually forgive me."

I sat back and exchanged glances with Elizabeth. Were we going to let him get away with that?

There are some things you just can't explain. Especially stuff about your family.

Elizabeth sucked on her lower lip for a second, then gave me a tiny nod.

"All right. I'll take sixteen apologies," I said. "How many do you want, Elizabeth?"

"Before we get to the fun part, I have to ask you

something, Salvador," Elizabeth said, frowning.

Salvador raised his eyebrows.

"Did you apologize to Bethel yet?" Elizabeth demanded.

Salvador nodded. "Yes. Absolutely. First thing this morning. She almost ripped my head off. Satisfied?"

"Okay," Elizabeth said slowly.

"I still don't get why she was so upset," I said.

"I do," Elizabeth said. "Nobody wants their crushes to be made public. I mean, no one talks about Jessica and Damon like that."

"Sure, they do," I said. "You just don't listen."

Elizabeth's eyes widened.

"You can get a big education if you hide out in a stall in the bathroom and listen to what the girls say," I said.

"I want a degree in that," said Salvador.

I punched his shoulder harder.

Elizabeth looked surprised. "Why were you hiding out in a bathroom stall?"

"It's not something I do every day or anything—" Ever since my older brother, Tim, died a year ago, I have these sad attacks every once in a while. If it happens during class, getting a bathroom pass is the only way to manage it. I'd sort of stopped doing it lately. "But if you're in there long enough, you can't help hearing things. And don't you dare say what you're thinking," I told Salvador, punching his shoulder again. I didn't want to hear one of his gross toilet jokes right now.

"Ow! Hey! This mind-reading thing is starting to drive me nuts! First Mom, now you."

"Your mom read your mind?" I asked.

"Yep. Just like you."

I smiled. I liked being compared to Salvador's mom.

"Anyway," Salvador said, tying his straw wrapper in a knot, then another knot. He glanced up at me nervously. "You know how the Doña always says, 'friends are like chocolate, there when you need them'?"

I nodded. "Yeah?"

"Well, I could really use your help. Both of you," Salvador went on, his face anxious.

"How?" Elizabeth asked.

"Today my parents' after-school activity of choice is a trip to the Red Bird Mall," he said wearily. "They want to buy me clothes. Terrible, ugly clothes."

"Last year you used the clothes they bought as your Halloween costume." I giggled.

"I was Monster Prep Boy!" Salvador exclaimed, smiling at last.

"He got a lot of candy," I told Elizabeth. "He looked cute, in a scary way."

95

Anna

"Kids ran screaming from me in the street. I drove away ghosts, witches, and vampires. And these were clothes my parents bought me to wear every day to school! So, I need you both to come and back me up when I try to convince my parents that Bermuda shorts and penny loafers just aren't me. Please, please, please come shopping with us?"

I knew Salvador was nervous about me and Elizabeth hanging out with his parents. But I was thrilled that he'd decided to risk it.

"I'm in," Elizabeth said.

"Me too," I agreed.

Bethel

"We're going to have company today," Coach Krebs announced before warm-ups. "Coach Fiedler is out sick, so the boys' team is going to join us."

Just when I thought I was safe.

Would this nightmare of a day never end?

All through afternoon classes I kept reliving the moment when I'd told Jameel to get lost. I couldn't wait for the weekend to begin so I could go home and hide out and sleep my way to oblivion.

Only a little longer, I had told myself. Only track is left. Running. You can forget about everything while you're running.

But not if Jameel was running with me.

The boys came out of the gym, with Jameel at the front of the pack. I ducked behind Jessica and Mary, which wasn't easy. I was taller than both of them.

"Welcome, men," said Krebsy. "Let's warm up with two laps, jogging comfortably. Then we'll stretch and finish with sprint work. Carry on." She waved toward the field.

It was crowded with all of us on the track at once. Ginger and Matt found each other and started talking. Lana jogged alongside Jessica, and they started talking about the Beach Blowout.

I took it slow, trying to stay in the middle of the girls' team, but they refused to stay bunched. Boys and girls got all mixed up.

Before I could do anything, Jameel came over and ran beside me. "Hey," he said.

I didn't respond.

"Hey, why'd you blow me off at lunch?" he asked, sounding more surprised than hurt.

"I don't have time for this. I have to concentrate," I answered coldly.

"Do you need to concentrate all the time?" he accused.

"Yes." I clenched my teeth. I was not going to say another word to this boy.

"Will you need to concentrate during the Beach Blowout? Wouldn't you rather just dance?"

"Would you please give it a rest?" I asked.

"No," he said. "Just say you'll come to the party with me, and I'll leave you alone all next week so you can"—we ran a couple of meters—"concentrate."

As we jogged on, I noticed that the other conversations around us had stopped.

What was this, a play? I glanced around.

People looked away, but I could tell they were listening to me and Jameel.

What was their problem? My life wasn't a spectator sport.

"Please, just leave me alone," I said quietly. I wanted my old life back.

"But I like you. Can't you admit that you like me too—at least a little bit?"

We ran on. I didn't answer.

"Time for stretches!" Coach Krebs called. "Everybody to the infield!"

"Come to the party with me. Just say yes. How bad could it be?" Jameel asked as we jogged over to the infield.

"Go for it, Bethel!" someone yelled.

Then they were all yelling.

"Give the guy a chance!"

"Come on, Bethel. Live a little!"

"What's your problem? Say yes!"

Anger raced through me. No way was I living my life by committee! Where'd they ever get the idea they could give me advice?

We started touching our toes and stretching out our calves and quads.

"Come to the dance with me," Jameel pleaded again in a soft voice.

I narrowed my eyes and glared at everyone still watching us.

They wanted to watch me do something? They could watch me do what I did for spectators. "The day I go to a dance with you will be the day you beat me in a race," I announced.

"All right, then! Let's race next Thursday after practice!" Jameel agreed, his brown eyes sparkling. He was totally up for this.

I guessed it was going to happen.

And I was going to beat him. He was speedy, but I'd been training hard. From what I could see, Jameel was kind of relaxed about training.

"Jumping jacks!" Krebsy yelled.

"Let's make it a four-hundred meter," he said, jumping up and down.

A sprint. I was a better distance runner than sprinter, but I was fast, and I had lots of endurance. I could work on my sprints all week.

"If I win, you have to promise to leave me completely alone," I said, panting a little.

"And if I win, you have to promise to go to the beach party with me."

I clenched my fists. *No way is he going to beat me.*

"Okay," I said. "Let's do it. Next Thursday. After practice. Here."

"You got it," Jameel said.

Everyone cheered. Krebsy had to blow her whistle three times to get them quiet.

Salvador

"Let's practice commando bad-clothes-aversion tactics," Anna said as we walked to my house after school on Friday.

"I don't know any of those," said Elizabeth.

"You are presented with a terrible clothing choice. What do you do, cadet?" Anna stared at me.

"Make a face?" I guessed, and demonstrated with my best "yuck" face.

"Absolutely not," Anna said. "You sidetrack. Say, 'Wait a sec—check out this one!' and grab the nearest acceptable alternative."

"Does that actually work?" I asked.

Anna stopped in the middle of the sidewalk and modeled what she had on, a pink tank top and a short black skirt. "Bad clothes? I think not."

"Cool," I said.

I appreciated Anna's spunk, but it didn't stop the roiling in my stomach.

Right now, I wanted to walk on past the Doña's house and end up somewhere else. Anywhere my parents weren't. I was convinced that bringing

Elizabeth and Anna home was going to mess things up with my dad. If I really wanted Dad to respect me, I could've invited Brian Rainey over and let him talk to Dad for six hours about sports. Dad would enjoy it, and Brian probably wouldn't mind. It wouldn't even be misleading unless I let Dad think sports was what Brian and I talked about when we hung out together.

Which, I guess, would be the whole point.

But Anna and Elizabeth were my best friends. And somehow that was more important than letting my dad down.

Anna ran up the Doña's steps, knocked, and opened the door. "Hello?" she called. "We're ready to shop!"

The Doña came out of the living room. "Anna! So nice to see you! And Elizabeth! How wonderful!"

My parents were right behind her. Mom smiled. Dad smiled.

What was I worried about?

"Hey, Dad, Mom. This is my friend Elizabeth, and Anna you know, of course. I thought they could come with us to the mall, if that's all right. Elizabeth, this is my mom, Marisol, and my dad, Fernando."

"Nice to meet you," Elizabeth said. She shook hands with my parents.

"This is a plot, isn't it?" Mom asked me. "You brought reinforcements. You're trying to out-flank us! Hey, Nando, your son is practicing strategy and tactics!"

"See what I mean about the mind reading?" I muttered to Anna.

"Hmmm," said Dad. He smiled at Elizabeth. Who could help it?

Anna grinned. "Mrs. del Valle, so nice to see you again," she said. "Mr. del Valle. We told Salvador we'd be his fashion consultants."

Fashion consultants! Did she have to say that? It made me sound like a supermodel or something! I wished Anna could read my mind just then.

"You're implying that I don't know what looks good on my own son, aren't you?" asked Dad. He sounded gruff, but there was a hint of a laugh in his voice.

Maybe everything would be all right.

"I think you see different clothes on a military base in Germany than you do in suburban California," Elizabeth said.

"What do you think of what he's wearing right now?" Dad asked.

Anna and Elizabeth scoped me up and down.

That's when I knew I hadn't thought this whole idea through far enough. There's nothing like asking your friends to tell you the truth about what they think of what you're wearing. I hadn't exactly dressed that morning with a clothes critique in mind. I was just wearing the usual baggy khakis and an oversized black T-shirt.

Oh, well. Might as well make the best of it. I struck a couple of poses.

"He looks fine," Elizabeth said.

"How can you say that? None of his clothes fit him!" My dad is the kind of guy who has creases in his pants and points on his collars even after a full day's work.

"But that's the style right now," Anna said.

"Just because all the other kids are jumping off a bridge doesn't mean you should do it too," Dad grumbled.

"Wearing fashionable clothes isn't the same as harming yourself," Elizabeth said.

I wanted to cheer! People never talk to Dad like that! Then I checked Dad's face. That vein in his forehead was throbbing again.

"Nando, why don't you go get the car out of the garage?" suggested Mom.

Dad gave her a frosty look but did what she suggested.

Mom, the Doña, and I sighed simultaneously.

Dad brought the car around front. We said good-bye to the Doña and piled in. Then we went to the mall.

Dad blew right by Space—my favorite store—and headed straight for McAllister's Men's Shop, which makes me think of guys smoking pipes, reading newspapers, and falling asleep in their tweed suits.

"Suck in your gut, son," Dad said. He held some navy blue slacks up to my waist and checked out the look.

"What happens when I breathe? None of my clothes will fit," I protested.

Dad smiled. "That leads to the next item on my agenda," he said gruffly. "Don't you think you should start a fitness program?"

"But I have gym every day except on weekends."

"It doesn't seem to do you much good. Make a muscle."

I wanted to sink through the floor. Anna and Elizabeth were standing right there, doing their best to keep their eyes averted. Red stained Elizabeth's cheeks. Another flaw in the logic of my brilliant plan. I didn't want Anna and Elizabeth listening in on this gem of a conversation. Too late now.

I sighed and lifted my arm so Dad could squeeze my bicep into nothingness, like he did every year.

"Nando, look at this tie. I think it would be perfect on you!" Mom said, diving to the rescue.

Dad let himself be distracted by the tie. It was

gold and blue and looked like silk. He tried it on and checked himself out in one of the little stand-up mirrors that lurked on the wooden clothes racks.

Meanwhile Mom frowned at the navy slacks, which Dad had handed to her. "Would you ever wear these if we bought them for you? They would look good on you, you know," she asked me.

Would they? I really doubted it. In fact, I was completely sure.

"Let me check with my consultants," I told Mom.

Anna and Elizabeth turned to us, proving that no, they weren't mannequins and they had heard every word. I wondered if my face would ever stop burning.

"Those pants?" Elizabeth asked tentatively.

Mom held them up to my waist again.

"Too formal." Anna shook her head. "Even our formal events are pretty casual. Actually . . ." She lowered her voice so my dad couldn't hear. "This whole store is way wrong for Salvador."

Mom sighed and put the pants back on the rack. "Nando, we're going," she announced.

Dad bought the tie and followed us out.

"Where should we go?" Mom asked our friendly native guides.

The next hour was painful, but not as painful as it would have been without Anna and Elizabeth. They headed for Space, and while my dad frowned at the blaring hip-hop and racks of cool clothes, I wound up with a new pair of cargo pants and two shirts I would actually wear.

"At least it was inexpensive," Dad said.

It's amazing how much money you can save if you stay out of tempting stores like McAllister's Men's Shop. I snickered silently.

We headed for I Scream! as a reward. Mom tried to drag me into Toy Joy, which was my favorite place on earth when I was seven, but I talked her out of it. Dad looked kind of disappointed. He's always had a thing for toy trains.

At I Scream! we all went to the counter to order, and then Mom and the girls went to find a table while Dad and I waited for the sundaes and shakes.

"Sally!" Mom called across the room. "Don't forget extra napkins!"

"I won't," I called back. *Great,* I thought. *Now the whole world knows me as 'Sally.'*

Just then, Kristin Seltzer and Elizabeth's identical twin, Jessica, came up to the counter.

Dad stared at Jessica. Then he looked back at the table where Mom, Elizabeth, and Anna were sitting, then glanced back. "Salvador? Who is this?"

Jessica's eyes glittered. She loves to call me names, and now she had a new one. "Dad, this is Kristin Seltzer and Jessica Wakefield, Elizabeth's evil twin. Kristin, Jessica, this is my dad." I glanced at Dad and saw that forehead vein of his working overtime.

Oh no, now what?

"Nice to meet you, Mr. del Valle," Kristin said, offering her hand.

"Gosh, *Sally*, you and your dad look so much alike!" Jessica smiled sweetly and fluttered her eyelashes at my father.

"Surprise, surprise," I said. Lame, I know, but my mind had gone totally blank.

"But we've got very different taste in clothes," Dad chuckled good-naturedly. "As we just discovered."

Kristin elbowed Jessica and smiled at my dad. "Salvador must be so happy to have you here," she said.

Dad and I glanced at each other self-consciously.

"I am," I said. "It's been really great."

And I actually meant it.

Top-Ten Stupid Parent Tricks

by Salvador C. del Valle, Anna Wang,
and Elizabeth Wakefield

10. Asking if you need to go to the bathroom—
    from across the room and in front of all your
    friends.

9. Asking you what you want to do and, once
   they find out, *telling* you what you're *going* to
   do instead.

8. Saying, "That's not music. That's *noise!*"

7. Asking for your opinion and then spewing
   out a list of reasons why you're wrong.

6. Saying yes when they mean no. Saying
   maybe when they mean no. Saying no.

5. Saying, "Put on your sweater. I'm cold."

4. Helping you with your homework, which
   means you have to do the whole thing over
   afterward.

3. Saying, "You're not going out looking like
   that, are you?" no matter what you're wearing or what your hair looks like.

2. Giving any explanation that ends with,
   "You'll understand when you're older."

1. Trying to turn you into a miniature them.

Jessica

The alarm went off.

Not now.

Yes, now.

No. Absolutely not.

I opened one eye, blinked sleep out of it, and checked the time. It was still dark. And it was Saturday morning. I could not think of one reason on earth why Bethel needed to start her extra training at *seven o'clock on Saturday morning*. She said mornings were best for running, but didn't morning last a while longer? Why couldn't we start at, say, eight-thirty? Why had I even agreed to help her yesterday? I must have been insane.

I groaned, got out of bed, and stumbled into the bathroom. Keeping the shower water luke-warm, I used my minty, invigorating shower gel, but it barely woke me up. Then I stumbled downstairs and ate some cereal. It was kind of spooky. Nobody else in the house was even awake, and here I was, up and dressed. I couldn't remember another time when *that* had happened.

I grabbed my gym bag and headed for the bus stop. It was cool and quiet outside. Not much traffic and still a bit of dewy fog. There were hardly any riders on the bus.

Bethel was jogging slowly around the track when I got to school, doing her warm-ups. I yawned and got out the stopwatch Coach Krebs had loaned me yesterday and the sheet of sprinter's exercises. At least I'd only be watching Bethel train, not running myself.

"Remember," I said. "Krebsy said not to overtrain."

"I know, I know," Bethel responded, flopping down next to me. She pulled off her training flats, got a set of spikes and a spike wrench out of her bag, and started loading the soles of her shoes with spikes, shorter than the spikes we used for cross-country. Then she hauled a set of starting blocks out of her bag. "These used to be my sister's," she explained.

I'd never tried starting blocks since they were for sprints. In cross-country we took off from a standing start. The blocks were made of metal and plastic, with curved pedals on either side for the runner to put her feet in.

"Okay. Let's go," Bethel said.

We walked down to the staggered starting lines for the four-hundred meter, just before the bend in the track. "First I have to figure out

111

which foot is my back foot," Bethel said, biting her lip in concentration. She stood up and leaned all the way forward. I thought she was going to fall on her head for a minute there, but then she took a step back with her left foot. "Guess it's that one," she said. She took the blocks and put the left one back. "Renee said I should try a medium start to begin with." She fixed the right block about a foot ahead of the left block and punched the spikes at either end of the block down into the ground, wiggling it to make sure it was set.

Over and over Bethel crouched on the blocks and then got up to readjust them. "I did this a few times when I was younger," she said, "but it still feels really weird. Want to try it?"

"Sure," I said. I thought I might as well see what it was like.

I crouched at the line and pressed my feet back against the blocks, then leaned forward on my fingers. It felt strange to be crouched and kind of trapped, coiled like a spring.

"On your mark," said Bethel.

I leaned on my knee, the way I'd seen sprinters do.

"Get set!"

I raised my hips and eased my shoulders forward. I could feel blood pounding through me.

The fog was cool on my face and smelled like mowed lawns and ocean.

"Go!"

I pushed off with my arms and legs and surged forward, rising as I ran.

I shot straight off the track.

I was so excited just to be starting from blocks, I forgot to watch where I was going. This race started on a curve. I had run right off the track and into the oval of grass in the middle.

"Whooee! It's Wakefield in the lead—that girl sure likes grass!" Bethel yelled, pretending to be a sports announcer. "Has she forgotten this isn't cross-country?"

I ran back to where Bethel was sitting. "Okay, Miss Smarty-pants, let's see you do better," I said.

For almost an hour she practiced starts, adjusting the blocks in all different ways and trying various methods of jumping off them. When she took a break, I tried it a few more times. There was something edgy about starting with blocks— the way it tilted you forward, like you were diving into the air or something. I kind of liked it.

We stopped for a Gatorade break, and I checked out the sheet of exercises I'd gotten from Coach Krebs. "Let's try some stretches," I suggested.

We did all our usual stretches and then a couple of extra ones off the sheet.

Then we tried three sprinting drills: quick steps, which are short, high steps with big knee lifts; kick backs, where you try to kick your butt with your heel; and leg drives, which are long, lunging strides.

"This is crazy," Bethel said, panting with exertion. "Why am I doing this again?"

"I was kind of wondering the same thing."

"Because I'm an idiot. Come on. Let's try pickups."

Pickups are variable-speed drills around the track, starting on the straightaway. First you start a slow acceleration, running at top speed for about thirty meters, then you gradually slow down all the way to a walk, and then you repeat the whole thing. I sat out, checking Bethel's technique against the pictures in the training book I'd checked out of the library yesterday afternoon. (There was no need for the librarian to be so snotty either. I'm sure I've used my library card more than once in five years.)

"I think you need to bring your feet up higher with each stride," I said. She trotted over, and I showed her the pictures.

"Huh?" she said. "You try."

I tried to run the way the people in the pictures did, but I felt like I was running like a chicken! I raised my knees waist high and kicked out my feet, but I wasn't going anywhere very fast, and I was sure I looked ridiculous. After one circuit I ran back to Bethel. "I have an idea," I said, getting my breath back.

"Yeah? What?" she asked, cocking her head.

"Lose," I whispered.

"What!"

"Just go ahead and lose. Go to the party with Jameel. What's the big deal anyway? You know you like him."

"Shut your mouth," Bethel snapped. "I will never, ever, ever lose on purpose. Come on, I'm ready for my sprint."

It took her eighty-four seconds to run four hundred meters. I was impressed.

"I've got to do better than that." She groaned.

Or what? I demanded silently. *You'll have to go to the party with Jameel? At least somebody's asked you to go. Unlike me, who has no one to go with.*

Training with Bethel

Sunday morning: Jessica's alarm goes off at 6:30 A.M. She groans, turns it off, and goes back to sleep. Half an hour later the phone rings. Jessica ignores it. Half an hour later Jessica hears a thumping at her window. She gets up and looks out. Bethel is standing outside, all sweaty from a run, one arm poised to throw her other running shoe at Jessica's window.

Monday morning: Jessica's alarm goes off at 5:15 A.M. She sleeps through the alarm, then wakes up enough to realize she doesn't want Bethel calling or throwing things at her window again. She gets up, takes the phone off the hook and puts the receiver in a drawer, takes a shower, and gets dressed. She misses the local bus but manages to run to the track by six-fifteen.

She and Bethel train until school starts. Jessica sleeps through all her classes, including lunch. When she gets home, her mother lectures her for putting the phone in a drawer.

Tuesday morning: Jessica actually wakes up before the alarm, makes her bus, and gets to the track before she realizes she's wearing the same clothes she wore to school yesterday since she was too tired to remember to lay out a fresh outfit like she usually does. She wants to run home and change, but Bethel won't let her. Training is more important. Bethel promises to loan Jessica a different shirt. She has several in her locker because she keeps forgetting to take them home.

They clock Bethel's four-hundred meter. She's down to seventy-nine seconds!

All the shirts in Bethel's locker are dirty too. Jessica washes one out in the shower and tries to blow-dry it. It's still damp by the time the first bell rings, but she wears it anyway and ignores the "nice-shirt" comments she gets on her way to class.

That night Jessica packs her gym bag with a change of clothes before she goes to bed.

Wednesday morning: Bethel's time is back up to 82.8 seconds. Jessica suggests that maybe she's overtrained. Bethel tells Jessica to keep her opinions to herself but then hastily apologizes.

Bethel flops down beside Jessica in the grass and pulls a candy bar out of her bag. She splits it in half and hands a half to Jessica.

"I've trained enough," she announces. "I'll be ready Thursday."

Jessica lies back in the grass, takes a bite out of the candy bar, and sighs with relief.

Damon

Something was definitely up with Jessica.

During lunch on Monday she barely talked and just smiled and yawned a lot.

Tuesday she wore this wrinkled yellow shirt. It didn't look like anything I'd ever seen her wear. And she'd pinned her hair up on top of her head, with strands of it sticking out all over the place. I'd never see her look so . . . messy.

I could tell she had something on her mind, but when I asked her what was wrong, she just mumbled at me. I wished she'd just tell me what it was.

Was she fighting with her family? That was always bad.

Or what if it was me? Had I done something wrong?

Maybe I should try to ask her again.

But what if nothing was wrong and I was just annoying her by asking what's wrong all the time and she told me to get lost?

Maybe this would go away on its own.

Wednesday at lunch I sat at our usual table. Jessica went through the cafeteria line, looking sleepy. She came over, set her tray on the table, and dropped heavily into the seat. "Finally," she said. "Finally."

Today she was wearing clean clothes, but her hair was still messy.

I couldn't stop myself. I had to find out what was wrong. "Finally what?" I asked, leaning forward with a worried frown.

"Finally," Jessica said again. She took her straw out of its wrapper and started sucking red Jell-O through it. After a minute she stopped. "It's soooo red. How come it doesn't taste red? How come it doesn't taste like anything at all?" She swayed in her seat and then dropped her head on the table.

Did she faint? I wondered, frantically trying to remember the CPR I'd learned in health class.

I jumped up, shaking her and trying to take her pulse at the same time. Jessica didn't wake up.

"What are you doing?" Ginger asked from the table behind us.

"She just collapsed! Jessica? Jessica?" *Okay. She has a pulse.*

"Here." Mary handed me a glass of water.

I splashed Jessica's face with it. That was definitely not in the CPR manual.

"Whoa!" Jessica said, opening her eyes. "I'm awake!"

"You fainted or something," I said. "Are you all right?"

She smiled up at me, still looking dazed. "So sweet," she murmured.

Lana handed me a can of Coke. "Try a little caffeine," she said. "I think she's just sleepy."

"Drink this."

Jessica yawned and chugged down the Coke.

A few seconds later she actually seemed a little perkier. I sat down next to her and grabbed her hand. "Jess. Please. Tell me what's going on," I said.

"I'm just tired."

"But why?" Was she working on some project that kept her up all night? Not likely, since she didn't care about grades very much. Maybe noisy neighbors moved in next door. I'd had neighbors like that. Was she having nightmares? What? What? *What?*

"I've been getting up at dawn every morning to help Bethel train for her race with Jameel," she said, yawning some more.

"What race?"

"You haven't heard?" Lana asked.

"Everybody's talking about it," Ginger explained. "Jameel and Bethel are having a race tomorrow. If he wins, he gets to take her to the party on Saturday. If she wins, he has to leave her alone."

"The training part is all over now," Jessica said. "So I'll be normal soon."

I studied her sleepy, beautiful face. There was a sticky, red smear across one cheek.

"Uh," I said, "you've kind of got . . . um . . . Jell-O on your face. From when you fell asleep. I mean, you really *fell*."

"What? Gross!"

I handed her some napkins, and she scrubbed her face. "Better?" she asked anxiously.

"Perfect," I said, wiping a little blob of red from her temple. "You look great."

"Go and See"
by Jameel Davis

Dark space goes on forever
Spreading out all around us
We race over a track of stars
Comets drag their tails beside us
Stars shoot past, singing songs of falling
We run side by side, holding hands
Only knowing we have to go and see
Go and see
We sing a song of falling
But we do not fall
Except for each other
Stars are our stepping-stones
And they go on forever
We keep running because
That's what we love.

Bethel

I took it easy at practice on Thursday afternoon, using the whole session as a warm-up.

While I was doing some stretches at the end of the practice, Coach Krebs came over and squatted beside me. "Bethel," she said, "you are a marvelous athlete with great potential. I've heard about your extra practices. I hope you won't keep sabotaging yourself like this. I have you girls on a season-long training schedule. Each part is carefully planned and needs to be adhered to. If we were heading into a meet next week, I would have absolutely forbidden the extra sessions."

"I know," I muttered.

"This will not happen again, will it?"

"No, it won't."

"Excellent." She smiled at me and stood up. "Good luck."

Good luck? Did she know about the race, then? I studied her face, but she just looked like her regular smiling self.

She must know. But she wasn't going to stop me. "Thanks, Coach," I said.

I got up, grabbed my gym bag, and went to wait for Jameel by the starting line. I was warmed up, relaxed and loose. I felt pumped and totally ready for the race!

The rest of the team should have cleared out by then, but they were still there, hanging by the fence below the grandstand, clearly waiting for the race to start.

All right, I thought. *I'll give them a race to remember.*

I reached into the gym bag to get my starting blocks, and my hand brushed a piece of paper. I peeked at it without pulling it out of the bag.

Every morning that week I'd found another note from Jameel in my locker, all poems. This last one was the best, even though it didn't rhyme. It was about two people racing on the Milky Way, side by side up in the night sky. When I read it, I could almost feel the stardust.

I sighed and got out my blocks.

Just then Jameel came jogging up, carrying his own blocks and looking as cute as ever. He smiled, and I had to clench my teeth to keep from smiling back.

Brian Rainey had agreed to act as starter and track judge. "You guys use the center two lanes, okay? Coin toss to decide who gets which lane." The inside lane meant a slightly shorter distance, but it meant a deeper lean around the curves too. Brian fished a quarter out of his pocket. "Bethel, call."

"Heads," I said.

He flipped the quarter. "Tails. Jameel gets the inside lane. Set your blocks."

Jameel and I knelt and spiked our blocks to the ground in our lanes. "Hey," he murmured. "Good luck, So Coy."

"You're the one who's going to need luck," I said. "And the name's McCoy, not So Coy."

"On your marks!" Brian yelled.

We backed into our blocks. I crouched, kneeling on my left knee. Then I lined my hands up with my shoulders, just behind the starting line. I pointed my fingers out, thumbs in.

Because of the staggered start, Jameel was behind me, where I couldn't see him. The back of my neck prickled.

"Set!"

I hiked up my hips and leaned forward on my hands, pushing my head and shoulders over the starting line. I studied the track ahead of me, breathing in through my mouth and nose, and tried to forget about Jameel, focusing my attention completely on the race ahead.

"Go!" Brian shot the starter's pistol.

I exploded out of the blocks and around the

first curve! Long, smooth strides, pushing off the ground with my toes and bringing my knees up high, my arms pumping close to my sides, hands cupped and loose. I leaned into the curve so I wouldn't run out of my lane.

I could hear Jameel's feet pounding the track behind me, but I tried to tune him out. Then he came even with me on the straightaway. *Run your own race,* I reminded myself. If I tried to get ahead of him, I'd lose it for sure.

I chased after my top speed, caught up with it about halfway down the backstretch, hit my stride, and relaxed into it.

Just think about maintaining your speed—don't let a fraction of an inch go.

We were neck and neck as we came into the second curve. I heard my breath sliding in and out of my mouth, my feet pounding the track. I leaned into the curve. Jameel ran a shorter distance, but he had to lean more. *Stop watching him. Just run.*

Out of the curve. Down the homestretch. Breathing hard, flagging a little, not used to such sustained speed.

No tape on this race, just a big group of kids watching the finish and Brian right there with his eye on the white finish line.

Jameel was ahead of me by about a meter, racing, racing.

126

Don't think about it. Just stay fast. Run your own race.
The ragged thud of our feet on the track, not quite synchronized. The creak of our shoes. Our breathing. Cheers and screams came from the stands, but they were muted, as though my hearing had shut down partway. I felt like I was running in a bubble. All that existed was me, Jameel, and this stretch of track we were on.

The gap between me and Jameel was closing. He was closer. Closer still. Beside me now.

Don't think about it.

I felt tired.

Don't slow down. Just keep running.

I wanted to stop.

Just keep going. Run through the finish line.

I leaned forward a little as I blew past Brian. Jameel was right beside me. We both kept going down the track. I let my speed leak out of me until I was running, then jogging, then finally walking. *Whoa.* I leaned over with my hands on my knees and let my head hang down while I caught my breath.

I straightened, still breathing hard. The afternoon breeze cooled the sweat on my face. I felt my shirt sticking to my back.

Then the sound came back on.

People were jumping up and down on the grandstand, cheering and screaming.

Screaming what? It was a wall of sound. I couldn't make out actual words.

I looked at Brian.

He was pointing at me and giving me a thumbs-up.

I glanced around to see if he was actually pointing at Jameel, but Jameel was about ten feet away, with his head down between his knees.

I won.

I won!

I *won!*

I had a mental picture of Jameel running beside me, his hands pumping like pistons, cupping air. I couldn't have beaten him by very much.

Maybe we could race again sometime. That was fun!

I smiled over at Jameel.

His eyes looked bleak. He bit his lower lip and started to walk back to the boys' locker room, his shoulders hunched dejectedly.

And then it clicked in my head, and I stopped smiling. It was a great race, all right, but I'd forgotten the prize: (*a*) no Beach Blowout date with Jameel, and (*b*) he had to leave me totally alone now.

I was free! People could stop making fun of me, stop talking about me and Jameel, and let me get back to my normal life!

So why did I feel like I had just lost?

Jessica

Elizabeth sat up in bed. "Why are you singing?" she asked me. She still had pillow creases on her face. It was Friday morning, and our alarms hadn't even gone off yet.

I stopped singing about what a beautiful morning it was, leaned closer to the bathroom mirror, and applied lip gloss. When I had achieved perfect coverage, I said, "Because I got to sleep in!"

Elizabeth groaned. "Six A.M. is not sleeping in." She collapsed backward and dropped a pillow on her face.

"Six A.M. is so much more sleeping in than 5 A.M. is. Bethel won! She won! She won!" I started singing again. No more miserable friend. No more early morning training sessions. Absolutely no more bad-hair days.

Plus it was Friday!

The big SVJH Beach Blowout was tomorrow!

Oh yeah. The big SVJH Beach Blowout—for which I still didn't have a date.

Or maybe Damon would have asked me if I could have stayed awake and didn't have Jell-O all over my face. I guess I wouldn't have asked me either.

I went into Elizabeth's room and pulled the pillow off her face. She squeezed her eyes shut.

"Why do you think Damon hasn't asked me to the beach party?"

"I don't know." Elizabeth yawned.

"Maybe he doesn't like me anymore."

"Are you kidding? He sat with you at lunch when you looked terrible. He even sat with you when you were asleep! Why would he do that if he didn't like you?" She sat up. "Maybe he doesn't have the money for a ticket."

Uh-oh. That hadn't even occurred to me. Tickets to the Blowout were ten dollars, and Damon didn't have a lot of cash.

I went to my room, grabbed my bag, and dumped everything in it on my unmade bed. Then I scrounged through the pockets of all my jeans. I'd been so tired after all the extra workouts with Bethel that I hadn't gone to Vito's or the mall after school for a week.

I managed to scrape together twenty-two dollars.

"Hey, Elizabeth, get up," I yelled. "We have to get to school early so I can buy some tickets."

Salvador

"Son!"

My eyes flew open.

I'd just gone to bed a minute ago. It couldn't possibly be morning yet. I glanced at the clock. Six-thirty A.M. Okay, it was morning, but just barely. I closed my eyes again. Just another hour . . .

"Salvador?"

There it was again—that sound. Maybe I was dreaming.

"Are you awake?"

It was my dad. He poked his head into my bedroom.

"Can I come in?" he asked.

I sat up, crossing my arms over my stomach self-consciously. I sleep in pj's—pj bottoms. I'm not used to having visitors. "Sure," I said, trying to keep from yawning.

Dad came into the room, wearing his burgundy silk bathrobe and brown suede slippers. He looked like a poster: The McAllister's Men's Shop Man, at Home, in Repose.

He sat down next to me on my bed, cleared his throat, and leveled his gaze at the wall just to the left of my right earlobe.

"I wanted to have a little man-to-man talk," he began.

I felt like a trapped wild animal. My shoulders tensed; my breath caught in my throat. I was cornered. There was nowhere to run!

"It seems to me you're growing up, son. And you're doing fine. You've got not one, but two pretty girlfriends."

"They're not—"

"Don't interrupt your father," Dad snapped. I loved his use of the third person.

"But—"

Dad held up his hand. "What you do is your business—I know that. But the only way for you to grow up to be a man is if you learn the ways of men."

I stopped trying to argue with him and stared down at the pattern on my comforter cover.

"Why don't you join a team, son? You'd make friends with other young men, build character and strength." He glanced up at the shelf where all his old school trophies were lined up, dusted and shiny. "It doesn't have to be football." He looked back at me expectantly.

I knew he wanted me to say something. And I

132

wanted to say something, believe me. But I was too scared I'd say the wrong thing. Besides, it was so early, my thoughts were all jumbled up. So I just shrugged, not meeting his gaze.

Dad studied me silently. Then he patted my knee through the covers.

"Think about it," he said, and stood up.

Thanks, Dad, I thought. *Thanks for starting my Friday off with a bang.*

Jessica

Now that I had a plan, all of a sudden I was nervous. I had two Beach Blowout tickets in my pocket, and I was all ready to ask Damon out. We were in the cafeteria, eating with a bunch of the girls' track team and some of their boyfriends—Mary was with Craig, and Ginger was sitting with Matt.

Damon was right across the table, looking extremely gorgeous, as usual.

I just wasn't used to asking boys for dates. Not that I thought they should throw themselves at my feet and beg me to go out with them. But . . . well . . . I wouldn't mind if Damon did that, actually. But why would he look at my feet when my face is so much better looking?

Don't be ridiculous, I thought. *Just ask him.*

I stared at my cafeteria lunch.

Putrid ham with mashed potatoes. The potatoes had an orange sheen. It was sort of remarkable. Remarkably disgusting.

I glanced at Damon's lunch. He had a

peanut-butter-and-jelly sandwich and some celery sticks and carrots. But for some reason, he hadn't started eating either.

My stomach growled. Gross! What if he heard it? How attractive was that? I popped the top on my milk carton and chugged down some milk to make my stomach shut up.

"Is there some kind of cone of silence over you guys?" Bethel asked. "Or are you having a silent conversation the rest of us can't hear?"

Oh, why drag this out any longer? The worst he could do was refuse. And then I would, of course, be seriously mortified and wish I could explode into a million pieces, some of which would land on his lunch so he wouldn't be able to eat it or anything else for at least a week.

I reached into my pocket for the tickets. They were kind of sweaty.

Damon frowned and bit his lower lip.

I pulled the tickets out of my pocket and thrust them toward him.

Just then Damon uncurled his fist. Inside were two tickets.

We stared at each other's hands. I could see the tops of the tickets in one of his. They had blue and silver SVJH stripes on them, just like my tickets did.

I leaned back, and we both started laughing.

135

Damon took a sip of his water and shook his head. "I wanted to ask you to this thing all week, but I couldn't get you to talk to me, and you kept falling asleep!"

"I'm sorry," I said, smiling happily into his sweet blue eyes. Those days were kind of blurry, but I knew I had been hideously un-me-like. And Damon still wanted to ask me out! I was so lucky, the luckiest!

"Today was my last chance!" He laughed again. "I've been helping one of my neighbors do yard work this week, so I had some extra money. I would have asked you last week, but I just wanted to be sure I could get the tickets together."

"Well, now we have a problem," I said, reaching over to steal one of his carrot sticks.

"What's that?" Damon asked.

"Who takes who out?"

Bethel

I peeked into my backpack just to make sure the pink piece of paper with Jameel's last poem, the one from yesterday morning, was still inside. This morning, when I opened my locker to get my books, books were all I found. When I went to grab my lunch, I checked the locker vents and even looked up on Richard's shelf to make sure I hadn't missed anything.

No poems. No notes. No valentine hearts or chocolate roses.

I had gotten what I wanted.

Only now I couldn't remember why I'd wanted it so badly.

I headed into the cafeteria. As usual it was couplesville.

Sure, the jocks had their own table, and there was the popular girl/cheerleader table. But most of the other tables were boy-girl, boy-girl—even the science-club table was coed!

I had that feeling again, the feeling that I was totally out of sync with everybody I knew.

"Hey, Bethel," Jessica called across the room. She was sitting with Damon, holding his hand! I don't think I've ever seen her smile that wide before.

"What's up?" I said as I approached.

"Want to come to the beach party with us?" Jessica burbled happily. "We have extra tickets."

I looked around the cafeteria to see if Jameel was there, but I couldn't see him. *This is stupid,* I thought. It was over, and I won. Jameel was gone.

Besides, I liked hanging with Jessica and Damon. I didn't mind being a third wheel, and they didn't seem to mind having me along. We could have fun. "Sure, I'll come," I said.

Jessica handed me a ticket and shook her head at me. I knew she knew what I was thinking. And I was grateful I didn't have to say anything.

I wished I'd never run that race.

Dearest Long-Lost Friends,
  I will soon be among the living
again. That is, if I don't drown in
parental attention before Sunday. I
will need debriefing, and you two are
the best men for the job. Please pre-
pare for many evenings of videos, pop-
corn, pizza, and stupid jokes. I
repeat, many.
  Until then, I remain your war-torn
soldier,
            Salvador

Bethel

On Saturday morning I got out of bed and then wondered why I bothered. My hands felt heavy, and so did my feet. I had trouble lifting my head. I felt like sleeping about ten more hours.

Drop the mood, I told myself. *You have a party to go to.*

Well, not for a while. The invitation said the festivities started at around four-thirty in the afternoon, and here it was, 8 A.M., so what was I going to do with the rest of the day?

Might as well do what I always did. Run.

But first I wanted to check something.

I got out all the notes and poems Jameel had sent me, plus the chocolate rose and the Blowout invite. Some of them I had to uncrumple. I couldn't believe how many of these pieces of paper I'd crushed. Guess I'd been pretty mad.

Not mad enough to throw any of them away, though. I uncreased one of the poems and read the words. Nobody had ever done anything like this for me before.

I laid them all out on the carpet and looked at them. Different-colored paper. Really nice handwriting. It all came together into a patchwork of Somebody Cares About Me. Why did I throw that all away?

I touched the last poem, the star-race one. *Go and see, go and see.* When I looked up, my eyes were blurry.

I pushed all the papers together and stuffed them into the bottom drawer of my desk; put on a T-shirt, shorts, and training flats; and ran out of the house into the soft morning.

Birds called from tree to tree. On lawns, sprinklers chattered and sprayed. A spaniel raced me for a block, barking. Cats lay curled on front-porch steps, watching the world with narrowed eyes. I jogged up this block and down that one, no plan in mind, but I wasn't surprised when I came to the track at school.

Somebody had gotten there ahead of me.

Jameel.

I slowed to a walk, then leaned against the fence next to the grandstand to watch.

He was doing interval training: a sprint around the curve, a slow jog on the stretch, a sprint around the other curve, a slow jog on the stretch, taking his pulse every once in a while to make sure he was exercising at the right heart rate.

He looked fantastic.

Suddenly he looked up and saw me. I waved. He started to wave back but stopped. Then he turned and ran off toward the football field over the hill.

He was doing just what I had asked for. He was leaving me alone.

It wasn't what I wanted. But that was just too bad for me. It was too late now.

Salvador

My parents were heading back to Germany on Sunday, so not long after lunch on Saturday, Mom rolled up her sleeves and took over the Doña's kitchen.

Except for the prep work—that she assigned to me. She gave me a bread board, a knife, and a huge pile to chop up—potatoes, carrots, a big onion, and zucchinis for the *albondigas* (meatball) soup.

She had things simmering and frying on the stove, pans laid out to put the enchiladas in when she had the filling cooked, and the tortillas fried and dipped in sauce.

Dad was grating cheese at the table near my slice-and-dice station.

The kitchen smelled like heaven. Spices, frying oil, meat cooking. It reminded me of life a long time ago, when I still lived with my parents.

"Whatever you do," Mom said, "don't you dare tell Mama I'm using canned chiles for the chiles *rellenos*."

The Doña was off at a dancing lesson with the

suave and debonair Mr. Fox, her dance teacher.

"Our lips are sealed," said Dad.

"She'll know, Mom. You can tell when you eat them." Canned chiles weren't as firm as fresh ones. They were more limp and wishy-washy, and they were more army green than pepper green.

Mom glared at me. "She may know, but as long as we don't tell her, she'll be too polite to say anything about it. If you tell her now, she'll rush out and buy fresh chiles and make me roast and peel them. I don't have time for that. Why aren't you chopping?"

I seized my big knife and attacked the potatoes, turning them into little cubes.

Dad grated furiously.

"You know, you can buy shredded cheese at the supermarket now," I muttered as I chopped the carrots.

"What, and defy tradition?" he muttered back, winking at me conspiratorially.

"But *canned* chiles?" I whispered in mock horror.

"Shhh! Whatever your mother cooks, it's always delicious," Dad said just loud enough for my mother to hear him.

"Of course," I agreed. I cubed the zucchini and began to chop up the big white onion. Then I remembered why I hate chopping onions. Tears streamed from my eyes.

"Don't rub your eyes! You'll only make it worse," Dad ordered. "I'll lead you to the bathroom so you can wash your hands and face."

Like I didn't know where the bathroom was in my own house? I blinked at him. And he winked back.

He steered me to the bathroom. After I washed most of the onion juice off my hands— the smell doesn't come off no matter what you do—Dad said, "Come with me, Salvador."

"Come where?"

"Out back."

I couldn't believe my dad was telling me to ditch kitchen duty! But the other half of that onion was still waiting for me, and I was still sniffing and tearing up from my first round with it. I wouldn't mind postponing round two.

We left the house and went around back to the grape arbor.

For a minute I suspected nothing. It felt perfectly natural to be strolling around the house with my dad. Then I realized that this wasn't something I did every day. Or any day.

Oh no! I walked right into this!

Another father-son talk.

I tried to put on my *Zone* head, the one where I could view any situation, no matter how embarrassing or upsetting, as potential material for comedy.

We sat across from each other at the redwood

145

picnic table. I wished I had some paper and a pencil, anything that would keep my hands and eyes occupied. Now he was going to go off on how to be macho and how macho men didn't have girls for best friends. Macho men had men friends. Macho men went out for every sport that came along, especially football. Macho men were always testing themselves for weaknesses and making themselves stronger by fighting with anything that would fight back until they could beat it.

Maybe he would talk to me about being a good soldier and having discipline and cleaning up my act. Be all that I could be: something a lot more like he was.

I *so* didn't want to hear it.

I already knew it by heart. Knowing it hadn't made me want to *be* it. I mean, when I was little, I tried to be everything Dad wanted me to be because it felt so good when Dad was proud of me.

When I was fighting everything, I kept getting into trouble. I wouldn't cry, but I couldn't win either.

Not until I figured out how to make fun of things.

I sighed and looked at Dad. Maybe this time I could just listen and not argue. He'd be gone tomorrow, and I could get back to my real life.

"You know," Dad said, "my father never understood me either."

Whoa! This wasn't in the script.

"I bet he felt just as frustrated looking at me as I feel looking at you."

Of course. I was my dad's idea of a total dweeb. Great.

"I bet you feel just as fed up with me as I felt with him," Dad went on.

I narrowed my eyes, studying Dad's face. Was he smiling?

"Your mother tells me you're never going to be like I was at your age," Dad said. He knocked on his skull. "I have a hard head. It takes a long time to get through to me, especially when it's something I don't want to hear. She's been telling me this for years, and I finally see that she's right."

I felt a strange lightness in my chest. I looked, really looked, at my father, with his regulation short black hair, his perfect posture, this intense energy he gave off, like a guitar string that's been plucked and is still vibrating. He wasn't a bad guy. A person could do worse than to be like him.

"Yeah?" I asked tentatively.

Dad heaved a sigh that sounded like it came all the way up from his toes. "I'll try to understand. I'm not saying I will, but I'll work on it."

I cleared my throat. "If you just pay attention to everything in your environment, you will find the tools you need. You just have to be creative," I said, quoting him verbatim.

147

My dad stared at me. For a second I thought that forehead vein of his was going into action again, but then he started to laugh. "All right. I'll keep an eye out," he said. "And one more thing. Your friend—Elizabeth?"

Uh-oh. "Yeah? What about her?" I asked, nervous again.

"I got the impression that you really like her."

I shook my head. "She just wants to be friends."

"That's a tough one," Dad said, and it sounded like he could really relate.

"Yep."

He came around the table and stood beside me. "When I first met your mother, she said the same thing. For years. Don't give up." He held out his hand. "Now, let's get back in the kitchen so your mother can tell us what to do."

I hesitated. "Dad?" I asked, looking up at him. "Yes?"

"Do you think you could help get Mom to call me Salvador instead of Sally?"

Dad laughed, his brown eyes shining.

"And I've kind of outgrown Lego, too," I added.

Dad nodded, still smiling. "I'll see what I can do," he promised.

I reached for his hand and let him pull me up. I felt lighter than I had in weeks.

Bethel

This was such a bad idea.

I had put on a dress, and I never dress up! I even wore stupid platform shoes. I felt like such an idiot.

Jessica had done my fingernails and toenails before her dad dropped us off. I had never used anything but clear polish on my nails before, but now they were metallic persimmon orange. They made me feel like I was wearing traffic lights on my hands. She'd loaned me some lipstick too. It was "cola berry" (or some silly name), so it didn't show up much against my dark skin, but she'd smeared shiny, glittery beige gloss on top of it, and now I felt like my lips were ten times their normal size. Then there was the mascara. Jessica said I looked hot.

How had she talked me into this?

As soon as Jessica and Damon and I reached the sand, I took off my stupid shoes and stashed them under a table. They headed straight for the dance floor.

It was a perfect day at the beach, sunny, warm, and a little breezy. The sun was just heading down. They'd already lit the bonfire, which seemed like overkill since it wasn't even dark yet. But I liked the smell of smoke and ocean.

A DJ spun up discs on a stage while couples danced on a sectional dance floor laid over the sand.

One table held drinks in clear plastic cups, with a woman behind it minding some coolers and pouring people what they asked for. There were three long tables with oilcloth tablecloths pinned onto them, but no food was out yet.

I didn't know what to do with myself.

The music was way too slow. I didn't mind dancing alone, but not to this kind of stuff.

I went down to the water and waded for a little while, watching the sun ooze into the water. Then I wandered back up to the edge of the dance floor and assessed the situation.

Jessica was still slow dancing with Damon, and they were exchanging blissful looks. Brian and Kristin hung on to each other. Ginger and Matt danced without touching each other, but they were definitely staring into each other's eyes, not noticing anything else. Mary and her boyfriend, Craig, were dancing too. Most of the people out on the dance floor were paired up.

Couple Hell.

Then I heard an inimitable laugh and turned my head. It was Jameel, standing with some of the other guys from the eighth-grade track team. He was wearing a nice, white button-down shirt and dark blue jeans. The other guys were taller than he was, but none of them looked as good.

I could stand here and feel sorry for myself, I thought. *Or I could call my parents and ask them to pick me up. Or I could walk over and ask Jameel to dance.*

I'm such a wild and crazy gal. Maybe it was the sunset, or the sea, or the warm sand, or the smoke of the bonfire clouding my senses.

I headed over, praying Jameel would say yes and not make a big deal out of it.

What if he said no? I tried not to think about that option.

A couple of the guys noticed me and started staring at me. One of Jameel's friends nudged him, and he glanced my way. Then he blinked and looked away.

I licked my lips, thinking I should quit before I made a huge fool of myself.

But hey. There I was in a stupid dress, with stupid makeup and nail polish on. Why be smart now?

I kept walking until I was standing right in front of Jameel.

"Hey, Jameel," I said.

He stared at me as though I were a ghost.

Had to be the nail polish.

"Hey, Bethel," Jameel said slowly.

"Would you like to dance?" I asked, forcing myself to look him right in the eye.

"What?"

I straightened up. "Would you like to dance?" I repeated.

"With you?"

I glanced behind me. Nobody standing there. "Yes. With me."

He shook his head like he couldn't believe what he was hearing. Or maybe he was shaking his head no. Okay, I could live with that. I had given him enough grief already.

"It was just an idea," I said, and turned away.

"Wait." He touched my arm. "Are you sure?"

I could see he was still hurt and kind of mad at me, and I wanted to explain and to tell him how much I really liked his poems. But not in front of an audience.

I grabbed Jameel's hand. "Come on," I said. I pulled him away from his friends and over to the dance floor.

His hand was warm in mine. As soon as we got on the floor, though, he let go of me and we just danced near each other, but not touching.

He was a good dancer, and I felt relaxed. I didn't care who was watching. Then the song switched to something slower. For a second we just stood there staring at each other, and then I put my hand on his shoulder. My palm tingled. Jameel reached out and put his hands on my waist, and I moved closer until I could smell the clean, laundry-detergent smell of his shirt. His arms felt warm and strong. All of a sudden I *wanted* people to watch us.

I thought I had all these things to tell him, but now I didn't feel like I needed to say them. Instead, when the dance was over, I led Jameel over to where my friends were standing.

"Hey, everybody. This is Jameel Davis," I said trying to sound confident. "Jameel, these are my friends. Jessica, Damon, Ginger, Matt, Brian—guess you already know him from track—and Kristin."

I waited for them to start teasing me, but they didn't.

"Hi, Jameel," Jessica said, holding out her hand. "Nice to officially meet you."

"Hey, Jameel," Damon said. "How's it going?"

The others said "hi" in an equally cool and mellow way. No teasing words escaped their lips.

All the tense parts of me relaxed.

The DJ put on that cheesy Aerosmith song that everyone pretends they're sick of but secretly love, and the whole group of us headed out onto the floor again. I leaned my head against Jameel's shoulder, and Jessica flashed me a thumbs-up sign.

Maybe this romance stuff wasn't so bad after all.

Check out the **all-new**....

....(Sweet Valley Web site—)

www.sweetvalley.com

New Features

Cool Prizes

The ONLY official Web site!

Hot Links

....(And much more!)

You hate your **alarm clock.**

You hate your **clothes.**

You're going
to love
Jr. High.